****

GIRL WITH THE MISMATCHED EYES

****

A Novel by

Bestselling Author

Jeanetta Britt

This is a work of fiction.
The events described here are imaginary;
the settings and characters are fictitious and not intended to represent specific places or persons, real or imagined.

Inquiries should be addressed to J. Britt
(brittbooks@msn.com)
Twelve Stones Publishing LLC
P. O. Box 921, Eufaula, AL 36072-0921
www.jbrittbooks.com

Library of Congress Control Number: 2021902308
ISBN: 978-1-7327071-5-3

Printed in the United States
First Edition

Editor: Fairrene Carter-Frost
Glorias G. Dixon
Cover: Michelle Stimpson

Scriptures from *The Holy Bible*
King James Version

SUPERIOR

©Jeanetta Britt

(from *Glimpses—poems of praise*)

I will call you superior when…
The diseases that kill me, don't kill you
You don't have a death date like I do
The vicissitudes of life that affect me
Don't affect you
Then, will I deem you superior

But, until then…
God is King
Jesus Christ is Lord
The Holy Ghost lives
And reigns
Inside His people

And one glad morning
We'll go home
Believers gathered around His eternal throne
And forever we'll sing our joyous song
Superior is our God alone…
Hallelujah!

Acknowledgments

I write action-packed Christian fiction. I write about the kind of world I'd like to live in—not a world without troubles, problems, and villains (nope, that's what makes life interesting and stories pop!)—but in a world where Christian people, seeking to please their Lord, make the journey just a little bit sweeter for one another. So, when you get a story idea for a deep dive into the many facets of modern-day racism—in a Christ-centered manner—you have to go with it—pandemic or no pandemic. Besides, you know the Lord will make a way. And He did. He allowed the words to flow; exposed homegrown extremists; put warped personalities on full display; preserved undisputable historical facts; orchestrated a lifetime of personal experiences and observations; and provided the dedicated time during quarantine (whether we wanted it or not) to develop an intriguing story. *Beware: Writers are always watching.*

The Lord also provided some spectacular partners. Many thanks to Glorias Dixon and Fairrene Carter-Frost for their confirming words: "Yes, this is a timely story that needs to be told." Thanks to Michelle Stimpson—the busiest bestselling author, educator, movie maker, and encourager—for producing a fantastic cover. Also, a shout-out to some sensational sisters—LaTanya Hunt-Haralson, Estella Washington, Barbara Rackley, Marie Lyles—and all of my readers, family, friends, fellow authors, and fabulous Facebook *besties*. Thank you for your strong and consistent encouragement. Your love, kindness, and support are very much appreciated.

Now, buckle up and enjoy this wildly inspiring ride!

****

"But when they deliver you up,
take no thought how or what ye shall speak:
for it shall be given you in that same hour what ye shall speak."
~Matthew 10:19

SUPERIOR

©Jeanetta Britt
(from *Glimpses—poems of praise*)

I will call you superior when…
The diseases that kill me, don't kill you
You don't have a death date like I do
The vicissitudes of life that affect me
Don't affect you
Then, will I deem you superior

But, until then…
God is King
Jesus Christ is Lord
The Holy Ghost lives
And reigns
Inside His people

And one glad morning
We'll go home
Believers gathered around His eternal throne
And forever we'll sing our joyous song
Superior is our God alone…
Hallelujah!

Acknowledgments

I write action-packed Christian fiction. I write about the kind of world I'd like to live in—not a world without troubles, problems, and villains (nope, that's what makes life interesting and stories pop!)—but in a world where Christian people, seeking to please their Lord, make the journey just a little bit sweeter for one another. So, when you get a story idea for a deep dive into the many facets of modern-day racism—in a Christ-centered manner—you have to go with it—pandemic or no pandemic. Besides, you know the Lord will make a way. And He did. He allowed the words to flow; exposed homegrown extremists; put warped personalities on full display; preserved undisputable historical facts; orchestrated a lifetime of personal experiences and observations; and provided the dedicated time during quarantine (whether we wanted it or not) to develop an intriguing story. *Beware: Writers are always watching.*

The Lord also provided some spectacular partners. Many thanks to Glorias Dixon and Fairrene Carter-Frost for their confirming words: "Yes, this is a timely story that needs to be told." Thanks to Michelle Stimpson—the busiest bestselling author, educator, movie maker, and encourager—for producing a fantastic cover. Also, a shout-out to some sensational sisters—LaTanya Hunt-Haralson, Estella Washington, Barbara Rackley, Marie Lyles—and all of my readers, family, friends, fellow authors, and fabulous Facebook *besties*. Thank you for your strong and consistent encouragement. Your love, kindness, and support are very much appreciated.

Now, buckle up and enjoy this wildly inspiring ride!

****

"But when they deliver you up,
take no thought how or what ye shall speak:
for it shall be given you in that same hour what ye shall speak."
~Matthew 10:19

Dedication

To the Sensational Class of 1971
Fisk University
In Celebration of our Golden Anniversary
Fifty Years of Love, Excellence, and Service
To our families, our communities, our beloved university,
and to one another

~

In Honor of Congressman John Lewis
Who forever lights our path toward love and "good trouble"
In service to humankind
Along with the innumerable host of
Fisk luminaries—past and present—
Who have and continue to do the same
To God be the glory!
"Her sons and daughters are ever on the altar."
FISK FOREVER!

PROLOGUE

Run, Gus, run! He panted, straining against his exhaustion to quicken his pace. The heavy footfalls of the deputy sheriff giving chase were matching his, stride for stride, and they were gaining on him—close—much too close. *How did I get myself into this mess!* Gus sprinted, lungs burning as though they would burst. His blonde hair was soaked under the black hoodie he'd worn to shield his identity. He stormed into his getaway car, gunned the engine, and sped away. *Whatever possessed me?* Gus' gloved hands pounded the steering wheel while he punched on the accelerator, demanding the vehicle to give him even more speed. *Whatever made me think we could burn down black churches and get away with it*?

Blue lights and sirens from the sheriff's cruiser were in hot pursuit. Gus bounced across the railroad tracks onto the white side of town in Screamer, South Carolina with a narrow lead. The deputy was gaining on his tail, and Gus' mind was caught up in panic. *I...I wouldn't be in this mess if I hadn't been trying to prove myself to everybody in town...the White Nationalist League...all those mean jocks and petty cheerleaders at ole Screamer High...and, oh, not to mention...the girl with the mismatched eyes.*

Gus skidded his getaway car into a narrow, abandoned alleyway; the one that he, and his 4-G Crew, had discovered when they were kids. He'd made sure the car's license plates were bogus. They couldn't be traced back to him. He jammed his vehicle into the tight crevice, killed the engine, and ran the rest of the way on foot. *I've got to get away! I can't get caught! I'm the law!* Gus' mind spiraled out of control. *But I will never, ever forget what I just saw!*

CHAPTER 1

Five Years Earlier

"Why do you do it?" Molly Anne Prichard's mismatched eyes flickered between Gabe Ingram and the three boys he'd just left to make a pitstop at his locker. As nature would have it, Molly's right eye was a clear blue, and the left one was a mossy brown.

"Do what?" Gabe puzzled.

"Hang around with those guys?"

"Those are my buddies," Gabe said as his friends ambled down the hallway, looking like three lost souls—Gus McVey, Greene Jones, and Greg Allen III. "We've all got one of these; you know?" He jangled his keychain so close to the girl's face it crisscrossed her bi-colored eyes. The keychain, bearing his prized G-initial, was Gabe's proudest possession. "We're the *4-G Crew*!"

"Yes, but you're not like them," Molly said, twirling her kinky, blonde ponytail. This was a conversation she'd wanted to have with Gabe for some time, but she knew it wouldn't come easy. "You're different—"

"Just because our lockers are side by side, Molly, doesn't give you the right to be my judge and jury." Gabe stiffened. "I've got a lot in common with those guys—"

"Just because all of you come from single-parent households doesn't make you joined at the hip, either." Molly flashed her two-toned eyes. "Those three clowns are losers…but you're not—"

"Those guys have hung with me when none of our stuck-up classmates would. We've been together since the third grade—"

"But this year, we're all graduating…*The Tenacious Class of 2010*!" Molly teased. "Well, I guess we're *all* graduating. Your friends rarely show up for class—"

"We're *all* graduating and on time!" Gabe eyeballed Molly. "I'll make sure of it—"

"See!" Molly said, making her point. "That's exactly what I'm talking about. You're the smart one. Those guys will only make it because you're carrying them. But what do they ever do for you?"

"Well, what would you suggest?"

"For one," Molly said quickly before the moment could pass, "you should come over to my dad's church." She raised her dainty white hand to ward off Gabe's fiery resistance. "And before you say anything, I'm not talking about the preaching on Sunday," she said, "but there're a lot of kids our age who come on Wednesday and Friday nights, and we have fun. We learn about the Bible, sure, but we also play games; plan for life after high school; and get to know each other better. Won't you come?"

"Me?"

"Yes, you!" Molly's eyes sparked multicolored flames. "Why not you?"

"But I'll be hanging with my crew—"

"Will you at least think about it?"

"Ok. Sure." Gabe squared his shoulders and slammed his graffiti-laden locker to cut off any further chatter. "Gotta go," he said and bolted to catch up with his three friends. Gabe rejoined the 4-G Crew just in time to run into the varsity football squad who saw it as their life's mission to crush them into the tarmac.

"Well-well…if it isn't the *4-Misfits*!" Brody Jansen, handsome quarterback, bombed a tight spiral while signaling an audible for his offensive linemen to position themselves for battle. Wise to their mean maneuvers, the 4-Gs attempted to make a hasty retreat, but the biggest of Brody's teammates had set up a blockade on the south end of the hallway, preventing their escape. Over the years, this kind of bullying had become commonplace at Screamer High, and the jocks and the pretty girls seemed to always come out on top. Screamer,

South Carolina was located in Nolan County, a sleepy little textile mill town, a stone's throw from the North Carolina border.

"Hey, don't you hear me?" Brody reloaded, and the popular crowd cheered. "Just look at you twerps! Do you get your clothes at the Goodwill, huh?" And everyone did look—and laugh.

Although the four boys had banded themselves together as the 4-G Crew, the bullies had branded each of them with far less flattering names. Like tall, nerdy Greg Allen III who they'd nicknamed *The Scarecrow* or, more often, *The Rich Kid.* There was geeky Greene Jones who they'd labeled *The Fat Boy.* And wiry, ill-tempered Gus McVey who they'd flagged as *The Minor* because he was only major in his own mind. And, then, there was Gabe Ingram who was handsome enough to fit in with the cool kids. He was tall with a brawny physique and rugged good looks, from the top of his red head to his thick bowlegs, but he wouldn't go out for football or any other sport that would make him popular; so, the cool kids simply called him *The Loser.*

"Naw, Brod-man!" Another bully cackled, stoking the fires to keep the fun going, "*The Rich Kid*, here, doesn't have to dress at the Goodwill. His daddy owns the mill—"

"Oh, that's right—"

"But his cray-cray granny over at the big house is turning him into a li'l punk—"

"Bookworm glasses—"

"Preppy blue blazers—"

"Cute li'l matching bow ties!" One of the pretty girls cat-clawed the remaining shreds of his ego.

"Yeah, but what about the other three—"

"Them?"

"They ain't got no daddies—"

"They got mammas—"

"Yeah, on welfare—"

"Ouch!"

"But could *anybody* afford to dress *The Fat Boy*?"

"Jelly belly—"

"Itty-bitty teeth—"

"He loves himself some pork rinds and grape soda—"

"Oink-Oink-Oink!" The cheerleaders began to rally in formation. "Oink-Oink-Oink! They sang while swishing their orange and blue pom-poms to the beat of the hysterical laughter from the crowd that was starting to fill-up the hallway.

Mortified, Greene Jones (*The Fat Boy*) tugged on his two-sizes, too-small tee to hide his belly button. He dug his nails deep into his own flesh to prevent himself from bawling like a blithering idiot. Greg Allen III (*The Rich Kid*) combed a shaky hand through his black hair, reset his wire-rimmed glasses, and sniffed back the tears in his misty blue eyes. Gabe Ingram (*The Loser*) kept an anchor grip on Gus McVey *(The Minor*) whose dark eyes were flaming like blowtorches. The 4-Gs had tried fighting in the past, but it had only gotten them kicked out of school. As the loaded trophy cases in the hallowed halls signified, the football players at Screamer High were unstoppable and bulletproof. But their proud tiger mascot, which governed over the powder blue walls, was silently bemoaning the whole cowardly affair.

"But guys...*The Loser*...well, he's really not so bad." One of the cheerleaders took up his cause, being attracted to his red hair and handsome good looks. "He just won't play ball is all—"

"That might've worked in the past, but it's too late. Now...this is all they're worth!" Brody side-armed a copper coin at the 4-G's feet.

"A penny! Whoa!" The crowd swelled in laughter that morphed into tears.

To the delight of his adoring fans, Brody gunned yet another strike into the 4-G's midsection. "But none of this may be their fault at all—"

"Not their fault?" the bullies chorused.

"No," Brody said. "Since their mammas will sleep around with *any-thing* in pants, they just might not be *white* boys after all! Who knows?"

"Yeah, who knows?" The hallway splintered into raucous laughter, dirty winks, and gritty high-fives.

Brody's final *Hail Mary* had sliced through the 4-Gs like a jagged edge because every word was true, and only Gabe knew why that particular accusation always hit poor Gus the hardest. Neither Gus, Gabe, nor Greene had a clue who their daddies were; and if their mothers knew, they sure weren't telling. Greg III knew his daddy, but his mother had died in childbirth, so he'd never known her; and neither had his grandmother, since her son had slipped off and married the mystery woman while away at college. Greg III had not so much as seen a picture of his mother and trying to talk to his dad about her was strictly off limits. However, it was the scar of their births that had bonded the four boys together since elementary school. But it had also given them a decided disadvantage when trying to deal with the relentless bullying they had to face each day. Fighting back was not an option. They had absolutely no ammunition.

The 4-Gs shrank to half their height—white faces flushed to a dark shade of crimson—as they clawed their way through the mean crowd to find relief. For as much as they'd tried to fit in with their classmates over the years, they had never seemed to hit the mark.

"And don't think you can just sneak by Molly Anne Pritchard," bad-boy Brody said, swinging his nasty words in her direction. "You don't get a pass either, Missy!"

"Well, what's her problem?" one of Brody's cronies said, setting her up for the put-down.

"A-dopted!" Brody announced. "Pedigree unknown!"

"Say what?" one of the pretty cheerleaders, who'd always been deeply jealous of Molly's easy good looks despite her obvious affliction, lashed out. "She looks white, but we don't know if she's a thoroughbred or a mongrel?"

"Yeah!" Brody agreed. "With her crazy-colored eyes and kinky, blonde hair, we don't know what in the alphabet-soup she might be." Brody pointed an accusatory finger in Molly's direction. "That white preacher and his wife adopted her to give her some respectability, but who even knows what their motives might be—"

"Yeah!" One of the pretty girls added a wicked wink. "Who even knows?"

Molly didn't respond to their taunts or even acknowledge they were speaking to her. She did her level best to rise to her full height of five feet eight inches; scroll her rainbow eyes up and away from the worrisome rabble; and sashay down the hallway with her head held high. Over the years, she'd gotten plenty of practice at doing just that.

"White Trash!" Another pretty girl jabbed a mean finger in her direction as Molly's pink Chuck Taylor sneakers rounded the corner.

"Well, look-a-here!" The mean jocks had their juices pumping, now, and they were about to go-in on a group of black kids who'd had the misfortune of passing by at just that moment. But, in the meantime, somebody must've complained about the commotion to the front office. The mob shifted slightly when Principal Morton came storming their way, but they didn't move; not until Miss Cora sauntered down the hallway in their direction.

"A bunch o' white kids…out here tryna play the dozens. Ha!" Miss Cora said in her quiet, plaintive style. "Now I know ya'll got much better things to do with yo' time than this, now don't ya?" And in just those few words, she managed to shoo away the cool kids and mean jocks like flies off a watermelon in the summertime.

Nobody ever knew why Miss Cora Lee Jackson had that impact on the entire student body. She was black, early forties, plain, and small in stature. She certainly didn't possess Principal Morton's authority or credentials, but she had the students' respect. Many of them never even knew her name, but from her lowly perch in the school's cafeteria they referred to her reverently as *The Lunchroom Lady*. Cora had always held sway with the kids at Screamer High; even before her brother, Bertram Jackson, had somehow lucked-out and become the first black Sheriff of Nolan County. *Who would've ever thought my brother could come up so far and so fast…and do it around here? Ha!*

Up on the north end of the hallway, however, someone was beckoning for the 4-G's attention. "Psst!" the young man demanded in a gruff whisper, swinging the 4-G's gaze away from the goings on with Molly and Miss Cora. They'd been equally parts glad and sad that it was Molly's turn to face the spoiled mob's music and not theirs. "Hey, fellas," the unknown voice persisted, "come this way."

"Us?" The 4-Gs hunched their shoulders at the stranger. "Whatcha want with us?"

"Don't listen to them idiots!" the stranger said. "Y'all is just as white as them snot-nosed brats. I can tell it just by looking at ya," he yapped. "So…let me show you something…something that's gonna get them uppity boys and sniveling lap-dog gals off y'all's backs."

The 4-Gs moved closer to the blonde stranger with the skinhead haircut, and he led them around the corridor to the next hallway. He was slightly older than the 4-Gs but not by much. "I've got an invite for you fellas," the young neo-Nazi said, beginning to make his pitch to the four he'd pegged as needy, gullible, and weak links—ripe for the picking. "It's time for us white kids to rise up! We've been pushed down for too long!" The boy's anger was rising with every word. "These right-wingers have crammed this black president down our throats…twice! So, it's up to us to keep these half-breeds and inferior races in their place until we can replace that spook with a real, true Aryan brother." The young man extended his right hand, tattooed with a red swastika, matching the black one on the right side of his neck. He clicked his heels and snapped a crisp *Heil-Hitler*-styled salute and shouted, "White Power!" Stuffing a tattered flyer into the 4-G's hands, he whispered, "This invite to the…White Nationalist League…is for your eyes only. See you tonight; 6 p.m. sharp. And boy-howdy, we're gonna change your lives!"

****

"That meeting was gangsta!" Gus McVey cheered along with Greene and Greg III.

"But it was a little scary, too, don't you think?" Gabe Ingram reasoned.

Gus McVey, 4-Gs natural-born leader, shook his blonde head vehemently. He had a wiry build with thick lips set into a perpetual sneer. "No, I don't think it was scary. I think it's just what we needed. We're white kids, too, and we need to learn how to stick up for ourselves."

Gabe nodded. But he also knew Gus talked tough to feed his own ego, while on the inside, he was a mess of insecurities and contradictions. Gabe vividly remembered the time when Gus had broken down in tears because he'd found a picture of a black guy squirreled away in his mom's dresser drawer. The worrisome find had left him devastated.

"Why would she keep *this* picture?" Gus had confided to Gabe in strictest confidence. "And keep it hidden no less?"

"That's just probably one of the guys from Billy's Biker Bar where your mom hangs out—"

"I doubt it." Gus had fumed. "They don't allow no blacks in that bar—"

"Yeah, but your mom's not in the picture with the guy, so it's probably nothing—"

"I sure hope you're right," Gus had said, face wincing in agony. "I'd sure hate to think that guy…this guy—"

"Could be your daddy?"

"Yeah." Gus' brown eyes had clouded over with fear and disgust.

"Naw! No way, man!" Gabe had reassured him. "Not with all that blonde hair of yours!"

"Look guys, we need to get our heads on straight." Greene's fat face beamed, bringing Gabe's mind back to the matters at hand. "Those bullies at our school are just stupid rich kids who have absolutely no idea who they are in this world—"

"Or what *we* are capable of." Gus set his thick lips into a wicked pout.

"And we're just lucky they invited us tonight." Greg III's blue eyes gleamed as he smoothed back his black hair.

"Did you see all those right-wing flags and swastikas?" Greene said, awkwardly raising the white-power hand sign they'd learned at the meeting.

"Yeah!" Gus said, returning the sign. "And did you see all the young guys dressed in camouflage gear?"

"Yes!" Greg III cheered. "And I talked to some of them, too. They're our age, but they don't go to school like we do. Their dads have taught them everything they need to know about survival—"

"They know how to shoot, and hunt, and prepare for whatever might come up…even the end of the world—"

"And they're not scared…not in the least. They're strong—"

"And ready and willing to die if it should come to it." Gus' chest swelled. "And that's power…that's the kind o' power I want!"

"They gave us beers!"

"Yeah, but not until after the meeting—"

"I guess alcohol and big guns don't mix, huh?"

"Yeah!" They all snickered like wicked little boys with their hands caught in the cookie jar. "I think we've found our clan!"

"But they didn't take us to the main compound." Greg III reminded them.

"Naw, this was just a recruitment meeting," Gus explained. "The main compound is deep in the woods somewhere. They won't let us see it until we've proved we can knock some heads—"

"You're right!" Greene said, in keeping with his fierce loyalty to Gus. "But, man, I sure would love to earn the right to see it—"

"Hang out with all our comrades-in-arms—"

"And finally have the honor to meet the Grand Master!"

Gabe Ingram was nodding his assent to his friend's wild enthusiasm, but he was beginning to have some serious reservations. For too long, the 4-G Crew had been force-fed a lethal cocktail of fear, rejection, and self-loathing; and, now, the WNL was offering them their full-fledged support to spew out all their pent-up hatred onto others without fear of reprisals. It felt like the perfect antidote. They could finally get the revenge they so richly deserved. But, for Gabe, the growing lunatic fervor of his friends was troubling and somewhat sobering. *They're starting to talk crazy! Gangsta! Knock-some-heads! Us? Really?* And with each passing moment, Molly Pritchard's invitation to attend her daddy's church was beginning to sound sweeter and sweeter.

CHAPTER 2

Five Years Later

As he got dressed in his clerical garb, the newly-installed Reverend Gabe Ingram could barely look at himself in the mirror. It was difficult knowing that he was the Assistant Pastor of The Church of the Evangelicals by day; and by night, he was a card-carrying member of the White Nationalist League, along with the other members of his 4-G Crew. He reconciled the two positions in his mind by convincing himself that the WNL was doing no real harm. They were merely a group of white citizens who were preparing themselves—and arming themselves—in the event of some national tragedy or catastrophe. Although deep down in his heart, he knew that wasn't true. While he fumbled with his tie under his impressive black robe, Gabe thought back to how far the 4-Gs had come in the five years since high school, and how he'd gotten himself into his current predicament.

****

Gabe couldn't have imagined how excited Molly Anne Pritchard would be when he accepted her invitation to attend the Spring Youth Revival at her daddy's church. In her frilly, pink bedroom, she'd tried on at least ten outfits to be sure she'd look her very best. As she prepared to leave to meet Gabe, Molly had admired herself in her full-length mirror—mismatched eyes and all. At birth, she'd had two perfectly bright blue eyes, but it was not long before her left eye had darkened to a mossy shade of brown. Her mother had been deeply concerned, but the doctors had told her there was nothing to worry about. Molly was diagnosed with a rare, yet benign, condition called heterochromia iridum that affects less than one percent of the population. The contrast between her bright blue and dull brown eye was stark and somewhat startling. The abnormality was her burden; it was her cross to bear. Between her mismatched eyes and her kinky, strawberry blonde hair, she'd become accustomed to not quite fitting in with the popular kids at Screamer High. But as she took a final twirl in her full-length mirror, Molly liked what she saw. But whenever she felt a little wonky about her appearance or how she measured up, she'd always think back to what her mother had told her in the second grade.

"But, Mommy," Molly remembered whining, "Patricia Emery says my eyes are funny-looking…just like my hair."

And her mother, Betsy Pritchard, had told her daughter something on that day that she'd never forgotten. "Molly Anne, we have to accept what we've been given. Your eyes are your very special birthmark from God. They make you both beautiful and unique. They'll make you be feared by some and loved by others. Only pay attention to the ones who love you."

Over the years, her mother's advice had seemed to suffice in her dealings with the prattling school girls who'd snubbed her. The boys, on the other hand, were mostly attracted to her. Her uniqueness was oddly sexy, like all rare things, and it made them want to get up-close-and-personal to take an even more intimate look. But, for the most part, she'd simply snubbed their advances. And aside from Sadie Potts, an older girl she'd grown up with at church, Molly had no real friends.

Out of necessity, Molly had grown accustomed to being different and spending lots of time alone. Given her circumstances, the world would whisper, "Be tough. Be hard. Be mean. Be as cruel to people as they are to you." But Molly had resisted the temptation; and, in her lonely hours, she'd resorted to reading her Bible instead. She was determined not to be a victim but a conqueror—an overcomer—and she believed in Jesus Christ she could be just that. For Molly, it meant making peace with her truth—her adoption, her oddities, her abnormalities. Moreover, it meant not struggling but accepting her circumstances. She was well-aware that other people had struggles, but theirs were often hidden while hers were visible for the whole world to see; and she had to deal with that. Letting things be—rather than trying to force or rearrange them—became the goal of her life. She believed she had the right to be fully herself because God made her just the way she was; He knew all about her; and He would always lead her in the direction He wanted her to go.

Molly's faith in Christ was teaching her to meet things head-on because His love for her was bigger than her fears and stronger than her foes. She knew, without wavering, that if everyone turned their back on her, Jesus never would. He would never betray her. He would never let her down. He would never let her go. She had His word on it, and she wore it around her heart like a shield. *I will never leave you nor forsake you.* Maybe, that's what gave her the nerve to reach out to Gabe and the 4-G Crew because they never quite seemed to fit in either; even though, their mothers and their skin were just as white as her own.

Gabe met Molly at her daddy's church each night of the five-night Youth Revival, and they sat together near the front row. Her daddy, Mike Prichard, had been Senior Pastor of The Church of the Evangelicals in Screamer, South Carolina for over 25 years; long before he and his wife, Betsy, had adopted Molly. They'd had no children of their own, and they treated Molly like she was the princess they'd always wanted. Nothing was too good for Molly. And, maybe, their unconditional love had given Molly the grace and kindness to reach out to a misfit like Gabe Ingram.

After a few nights of *Hallelujah-Praise-the-Lord* sessions, Gabe was hooked. Listening to the preachers proclaim the Gospel and tell of the unfailing love of Jesus had filled him with a newfound sense of hope. Gabe was drawn with the simplicity of childlike faith, and he enjoyed the comforting order of things that the church had to offer. He liked the idea of the church's established hierarchy, and he could see himself fitting into it someday—*finally, fitting in somewhere.* During the Revival, the gleam in Molly's eyes had stirred a distant place in Gabe's heart as well; and in what seemed like no more than a moment, he'd fallen deeply in love with her, too.

"I think I'm falling in love with Molly Prichard," Gabe confided to his fellow members of the 4-G Crew.

"What?" Greene's pork-rind face scrunched into a knot. "Why would you wanna go and do a thing like that, dude?"

"Yeah, why?" Gus snarled, sounding like a full-fledged member of the WNL. "You don't even know this girl. She's a-dopted...and her pedigree is questionable. She's got kinky, blonde hair and mismatched eyes; who knows who her people really are? So, I, for one, do not think it's a very good idea."

"Well, it does sound a bit hasty," Greg III said, sounding nerdy as always. "We're barely graduating high school, here, and you're talking about getting married. What will you possibly do to support yourself and a wife?"

"I could work!" Gabe protested. "You'd help me get a job over at your daddy's textile mill; wouldn't you, Greg III?"

Despite the reluctance of the 4-G Crew, Gabe pressed on, and he proposed to Molly on graduation night at Screamer High. He dropped to one knee as she crossed the stage, high school diploma in hand, and asked her. "Molly Prichard, I love you...I love you like you're a piece of myself...and I always will," he vowed. "Will you marry me?"

Gabe didn't have a ring to offer her, but the brilliant gleam of hope and love in his eyes was enough for Molly. And just as excitedly—with eyes lighting every color of the rainbow—she'd said, "Yes! Yes! Oh, my God! Yes!"

Of course, Gabe didn't have all the answers to the questions the 4-G Crew had raised, but he'd established a great rapport with Molly's mom and dad over the months he'd attended their church.

As a result, he and the pastor were able to sit down and give the matter some serious consideration.

"I think the two of you are a might young to be discussing marriage," Senior Pastor Mike Pritchard said.

"I know, sir," Gabe agreed. "We are, but I'm committed to a life with Molly."

"That said," the pastor continued, "if the two of you are committed to marriage, there are some steps you need to take first."

"Oh?"

"Yes." Molly's dad firmed. "First off, you'll need to go through premarital counseling with me and some of the deacons."

"Okay." Gabe gave him a stiff nod.

"And," the pastor went on, "you've got to be able to take care of yourself and a wife. That takes education—"

"But I can get a job at the textile mill. My good friend's daddy owns it, and he—"

"Don't resist me on this one, son." Pastor Pritchard raised his hand to ward off further protest. "Just listen."

"Yes, sir."

"I've noticed the sincerity with which you delve into God's word, and I could suggest a good seminary for you. And, maybe when you're done, you could come back here and be a minister…or even my Assistant Pastor—"

"You think?" Gabe gaped. It was true. He had certainly developed a hunger for the Bible and the teachings of the church since getting to know Molly and her family.

"And I know Molly has always wanted to go to a four-year college so that she can teach elementary school kids," her dad said. "So, in four years, both of you will have finished your education and be ready to start a life together—"

"Four years?" Gabe moaned. "But that's a lifetime—"

"And if your love for each other can't endure four years apart, then it's not worth having…it's not real."

"I guess so." Gabe sobered. "But I'd have to ask Molly about all this—"

"Of course!" Pastor Pritchard rose, slapping one knee. He was a squat man with a round, balding head and squinty brown eyes, but he was known in the community for his heart of gold. "The two of you talk it over, but I won't be able to give you my blessings unless you two decide on the course of action I've laid out here today. In the meantime, I'll talk it over with my wife, too, and we'll all try to get on the same page. How's that?"

"I guess that's fair." Gabe shook the pastor's hand as though he were a man of his word. He felt pretty confident about the approval of Molly's mom. Betsy Sue Pritchard was a sweet-hearted, plain woman—yet, too beautiful for the likes of the pastor—and they had hit it off from the beginning. It was her kind and gentle spirit that had made Gabe confident that a life with the daughter she'd raised as her own could be nothing short of wonderful.

The rest of the 4-G Crew never liked the idea of Gabe getting married, especially to Molly, but they'd relented as long as he'd promised to continue to attend the clandestine White Nationalist League meetings with them. Their unit's meetings were held once a week at night at the hideout they'd been introduced to on their first meeting. They'd not been permitted to visit the main compound that was deep in the woods bordering North Carolina, at least not yet. But they were anxious to gain the trust of the local unit and be given the privilege to finally meet the Grand Master of the WNL.

So, in the five years since high school, the 4-G Crew had stayed in lock-step with each other through their loyal kinship and their affiliation with the WNL. Greg Allen III (*The Rich Kid*) was proving himself in the family business. Allen Textile Mills, Inc. was proud of its role as the largest employer in Nolan and surrounding counties. Greg III was expected to work his way up through the ranks like his grandfather, Greg Sr, and his daddy, Greg II, who was the current CEO. Greg III started out as a lowly stock clerk and had worked his way up to the Manager of Purchasing, with an eye on the front office. But his daddy probably would've stopped him dead in his tracks if he'd known that Greg III was hooked-up with a radical hate group like the WNL.

Surprisingly, Greene Jones had done better for himself since high school than anyone would've expected. He'd always been good with his hands and loved computer games and such, but he'd also developed quite a rich speaking voice over the years. Maybe, it was from all the fat hanging around his jowls. But while doing some contract work to repair the computer system at the local radio station, WSCR, Greene was overheard testing the mike system by the owner. His voice was so impressive that the owner offered him a job on the spot—as a disc jockey. *What? The Fat Boy—a star on the local radio station in Screamer? Welp…there you have it!* Greene was an instant success. He hosted a hit late-night jazz show—Jazz on the Greene—as well as, the daily Christian radio talk show that often reported the goings on at The Church of the Evangelicals. Since Greene had no family left—his mother had moved to Screamer from Detroit, and she'd died shortly after his high school graduation—his connection with the 4-Gs and the WNL were his sacred lifeline.

And what of Gus McVey (*The Minor*)? He'd put his aggressive nature to work at the Nolan County Sheriff's Office. He was a lowly deputy, now, but he had his sights set on being the sheriff one day; and he didn't mind whipping a few heads along the way to get it done. Besides, with the backing of the WNL, he figured he'd be a shoe-in for the job. Gus had quickly become the WNL's *man-downtown*—their secret agent; their ace-in-the-hole—and his standing in the local unit was growing by leaps and bounds. The other 4-Gs realized that if they'd ever be trusted enough to see the main compound and meet the Grand Master, it would be in large part attributable to Gus' clout and comradery with the rest of the hard-core militants in their unit.

****

Now Gabe Ingram (*The Loser*) found himself, some five years since high school, standing in the mirror as Assistant Pastor of The Church of the Evangelicals and married to the love of his life, Molly Anne Pritchard Ingram. And he was delighted that Molly was getting to live out her dream; she was teaching third graders at Screamer Elementary. But his heart sank a little bit every time he thought about his secret double life with the WNL. *How would Molly, or her parents, feel about me if they knew? What would they say if they knew that a minister of the gospel was mixed-up with a hate group like the White Nationalist League?*

Their church catered to nearly an all-white congregation, but mixing of the races was not expressly prohibited. There was a sprinkling of black and brown members, not the least of which was the newly-elected, first black Sheriff of Nolan County, Bertram Jackson, and his wife, Lucille.

"We are just *very good people*…trying to protect our own kind," Assistant Pastor Gabe Ingram muttered to himself as he finished his preparations for the pulpit. But, for the life of him, he could not raise his eyes to face the man in the mirror.

CHAPTER 3

Folks in Screamer and Nolan County were still scratching their collective heads as to how they ended up electing a black sheriff in the last election. Everyone surmised, maybe, it had something to do with the fact that Bertram Jackson, then a lowly deputy on the force, had saved a little white girl from drowning. The little, towheaded four-year-old had somehow gotten separated from her parents at Nolan State Park which warranted an all-out manhunt for her whereabouts. When Deputy Jackson had come upon the little girl, she was dangerously suspended by a broken tree branch over a gaping gorge filled with the muddy backwaters of the raging Congaree River. Somehow, Bertram Jackson had sweet-talked the little girl and prevented her from panicking and plunging to her certain death. He then roped himself to his service Bronco and rescued the little girl, bringing her safely back to her parents.

Deputy Bertram Jackson was treated to a parade that was replete with all the high school bands and majorettes in Nolan County. Standing on the elevated platform, which was draped in the red-white-and-blue, Screamer's Mayor Buzz Underwood presented the deputy with a meritorious conduct award and the keys to the city while the grateful parents of the little girl wept and cradled her in their arms in the front row. Sheriff Lester Magpie stood alongside the festivities, chest swollen with pride, excited that his department was finally in the limelight for a good thing.

Jackson's black face was plastered on every front page of the local *Screamer Times* for weeks that summer leading up to the election. Headlines, like *Hail to Our Hometown Hero* and *Deputy Bertram Jackson—A Man for All the People*, were seen everywhere. The newspaper articles would go on to recite his local prominence as a football player at Screamer High; his steady rise through the ranks of the Sheriff's Department since graduation; his marriage to Senior Class Queen, Lucille; and his status as an all-around good guy in Nolan County.

Mrs. Lucille Jackson seized on the moment. She swung into action to strike while the iron was hot. She'd been waiting for her opportunity to make her husband shine and to ride in victoriously on his coattails, and she was going to use Screamer's close-knit black community to get the job done.

Given her new-found influence, Lucille, dressed in her finest red suit and pumps, revealing more than a modicum of cleavage, sashayed into every business on Screamer's Town Square with the same salutation. "Good morning, I'm Mrs. Lucille Jackson, wife of hometown hero, Deputy Bertram Jackson. May I have a brief word with your manager?" And when she'd get the poor, unsuspecting store managers behind closed doors, Lucille would lay it on thick. She would either convince the business to donate to one of her causes in the black community or sponsor an activity.

On one such occasion, Lucille had met with some stiff resistance when word of what she was doing had spread through the businesses on the Square like wild fire. "May I speak with your manager?" Lucille had requested.

"No. I'm sorry he's unavailable." The young, blonde receptionist presented her with firm resolve and a stone face.

"Do you know who I am?" Lucille slung back her own blonde-streaked weave over her slender, nut-brown face. "I'm Mrs. Bertram Jackson. My husband is our hometown hero who saved that little white girl from certain destruction, and I don't think you want it said that your store manager could not spare even a few minutes of his very precious time to speak with me about a matter of utmost importance." Lucille turned on her heels as if to leave while throwing a side-eyed admonition at her adversary. "But…if that's the case, young lady, I will be sure to let my newfound friends at the newspaper know—"

"But…but—" the wilted receptionist stuttered. "Wait! Wait right here! I'll get Mr. Dixon to come right out."

"See that you do!" Lucille stiffened her posture. While on her self-proclaimed mission, she curried no favors and took no prisoners.

Lucille leveraged sponsorships and cash donations from the white businesses on the Square to meet some vital needs in her community. Screamer's black community was located across the railroad tracks, south of downtown. Ann Street was its spine, flanked by a trio of streets the locals affectionately called, *The Presidents*—Washington, Lincoln, and Jefferson. If somebody said they lived in *The Presidents*, folk knew they lived on the black side of town, without having to get too specific. Ann Street and The Presidents were crossed by numbered avenues, starting with 1st Avenue at the railroad tracks. However, on the north side of the tracks—the white side—all of the uptown avenues had been graced with unforgettable names, like Magnolia, Rosebud, and Sweetgum.

From the war chest she accumulated, Lucille bankrolled fish fries and bingo games at the community center in The Presidents to lure the adult and senior citizen voters. She also sponsored King and Queen contests, as well as, little league football and softball teams for the kids. The backs of their team jerseys might have borne the logos of the businesses she'd strong-armed, but all of them carried the exact same message: *In Honor of Deputy Bertram Jackson—Hometown Hero.*

It was too late to get her husband's name on the November ballot, but Lucille did everything in her power to keep his name in the forefront of the minds of black voters before the upcoming 2014 election. Besides, she didn't want to put his job at risk because Sheriff Magpie had been entrenched in the office for nearly 25 years. And if Bertram were to lose in a head-to-head contest against the white incumbent, he would surely forfeit his job as deputy and, maybe, his standing in the community. And Lucille was having none of that.

When she felt her efforts were gaining traction with the black voters, Lucille stepped up her game. She partnered with the NAACP, Urban League, and the Retired Teachers' Association to sponsor voter registration drives and get-out-the-vote campaigns. She urged them to get their members and the community to write-in her husband's name on the ballot come November. Of course, the *Write-In Campaign* was strictly hush-hush in the black community, but it would prove to be very effective.

At her home church, Beulah Bible, Lucille softened Pastor Early Lee Renfrow to support her husband's rise to sheriff. "Pastor Renfrow, if you take the lead, you know the other two churches will follow." Lucille set out to schmooze him in a closed-door meeting. She'd wrangled the meeting out of his secretary, Sister Sara, when she'd winked at the rigid gatekeeper and whispered, "And about that *li'l ole thang*…well, it can stay just between the two of us." Lucille hinted that she knew the secretary's dirty little secret, while in reality, she didn't have the slightest clue. But she figured everyone had at least one; and, evidently, she'd been right.

"Now, what are you saying, Sister Jackson?" Pastor Renfrow pretended to be slow on the up-take as he presided behind his massive, mahogany desk, but he knew well the woman with whom he spoke. She'd been in his congregation since birth, and it was well-known that her family members were of the tricky sort.

"You know what I'm saying, Pastor," Lucille said in her softest tone, settling into the stiff guest chair. The pastor liked it that way so folk wouldn't find it comfortable to linger in his presence.

"No." Pastor Renfrow resisted. "Enlighten me."

"Well, alright." Lucille crossed her long, shapely legs at the knee. For the occasion, she'd made sure her short skirt and makeup were on point. "You're the only one in town who can talk to the preachers over at Holy Ghost Headquarters and Mount Olive and get them to move." Holy Ghost Headquarters was a storefront church on Ann Street and 1st Avenue, down near the railroad tracks, while Mount Olive housed a slightly larger congregation on Lincoln and 3rd Avenue. However, Beulah Bible was the crown jewel of the black churches in Screamer, proudly located on Jefferson and 5th Avenue—in the heart of the black community—for over 100 years.

"Well, what do you want us to do?" Pastor Renfrow knotted his brow. "You know we can't get too involved in politics from the pulpit—"

"I know that." Lucille smiled and flung back her blonde-streaked curls over a face that was flirting with middle age. "And I would never ask you to do a thing like that—"

"Uh-huh—"

"All I'm asking," Lucille stated, "is that you allow us to work with our membership to set up voter registration tables after every service, and we can teach the voters how to write-in Bertram's name—"

"And get the other two churches to do the same?"

"Yes." Lucille shrugged. "You know those two churches have been feuding for years—"

"I know." The pastor shook his head woefully. "Ever since Mount Olive got a woman pastor."

"And you know you're the only one they'll listen to—"

"But—"

"But Bertram and I have attended Beulah Bible all of our lives, and he's one of your most trusted deacons, Pastor." Lucille tightened her gaze. "He deserves your support."

"Well, I guess you're right." Pastor Renfrow relented. "I guess I could try talking to Bishop Pride over at Holy Ghost Headquarters, and Pastor Shaundra Strong at Mount Olive—"

"You won't have to do a thing, Pastor." Lucille hurried to her close. "I'll work with our Ladies' Aide Society to get things handled here at Beulah Bible, and I'll set it up with the other churches, too…as soon as you give me the green light."

"Well, alright, Sister Jackson." The pastor shook his head. "Alright."

Leading up to the election, all three churches ran voter registration drives after every service. In addition, the trained volunteers from the combined civic groups instructed all voters—new and old—how to write-in Bertram Jackson's name on the ballot when the time was right.

Bertram, on the other hand, was a little embarrassed by his wife's all-out campaign to get him elected sheriff. He was a humble man at heart, but he also believed he was the right man for the job. Besides, he knew Lucille's efforts were primarily self-serving so that she could become one of the leading ladies in Nolan County—black or white. Nonetheless, he dearly loved his wife, and he always found a way to overlook her selfish ambition.

In November, Lucille's plan had worked like a dream. She'd expected that most of the white voters would sit this one out since Sheriff Lester Magpie was running unopposed, and they didn't much care. The Sheriff was fat, old, lazy, and with too many bad raps on his record for pestering the young ladies over the years. And since he was on his proverbial last leg with no viable opponent with which they could give him the boot, the majority of the white citizens of Nolan County simply did not turn-out to vote. Hence, Bertram Jackson squeezed in as the lone write-in candidate. And before you could say, *hot-fish-and-grits*, Screamer and Nolan County, South Carolina had a black sheriff—the first one of his kind in the history of the region.

CHAPTER 4

The election turned out to be a good thing and a bad thing for the nefarious 4-G Crew. Of course, the White Nationalist League, of which they were now full-fledged members, hated the fact that Jackson—a black man—had won the election. Nevertheless, it did give one of their own an opportunity to move up in the ranks to Chief Deputy—none other than Gus McVey. And from the very beginning, the WNL began strategizing how they could discredit Bertram Jackson and replace him in the next election with their own, Chief Deputy Gus McVey. This goal soon became the first and most-prized agenda item at every WNL meeting.

From the first, the 4-G Crew began to assess what they could bring to the table to reach their goal of discrediting Sheriff Jackson and electing their buddy. If they could pull this off, no one would be able to refer to Gus as *The Minor*—no, not ever again. But, more importantly, they knew it would elevate their standing with the WNL; and, maybe, give them the chance they all wanted to be introduced to the Grand Master at his deep-woods compound.

For Reverend Gabe Ingram, the answer was simple. He brought with him all the community connections that The Church of the Evangelicals had to offer. Unbeknownst to his father-in-law, Senior Pastor Pritchard, a number of WNL members were in his congregation, and some even filled key slots on the leadership team, but Gabe knew them all. Of course, Chief Deputy Gus McVey's position was solidified as the prospective candidate, and his role was to keep a tight eye on the black sheriff until they could kick him out. Since everyone in Screamer and Nolan County knew Greene Jones as the loyal and trusted voice of WSCR, Greene was solidly in as the community influencer. He was the steady voice of high school football under the Friday night lights; the smooth voice that brought soothing Christian radio into the homes of the devout; and the last voice the lovelorn heard under the stars on late night jazz radio. Pretty much anything Greene said on the radio would be taken as gospel.

"We know what we're bringing to the table to takedown Jackson," Gus said as he circled his index finger from himself, to Gabe, to Greene. They'd chosen the last picnic table alongside Nolan Lake as their secret meeting spot, and they were all hunkered down there in honor of the first day of spring. "But what are *you* willing to do for the cause?" All eyes fell on Greg III. And this was the moment of reckoning because they knew he had the most to lose.

"Who me?" Greg III added a shrug to his weak smile.

"Yeah, you!" the trio sang out.

****

Allen Textile Mills, Inc. was the largest employer in Nolan and surrounding counties. They turned the cotton grown in the region into fine bedding and other sought-after textile products. And as CEO, Greg II, was proud that he'd been able to cultivate global markets for their fine products over the years.

Like his daddy before him, Greg II insisted that his son learn the business from the ground up. So, while he was attending Screamer Community College, Greg III was also working as a clerk in the receiving department. And, in the five years since high school, he'd worked his way up the ranks to Manager of Receiving. The president of the company, and his daddy's most trusted employee, would be retiring soon, and Greg III knew if he played his cards right, he had a great shot at filling the vacant slot.

Greg III's family lived in the biggest house in Nolan County on the outskirts of Screamer. Back in the days before his grandfather, Greg Sr., had purchased the 200-acre site, it had been part of a working cotton plantation. But, as soon as Greg III graduated high school, he vacated the big house and took up the little cottage in back that had been the housemaid or slave quarters in the old days. Greg III had made the move primarily to get from under the clutches of his grandmother, Elsie Louise Allen, but his dad still shared the big house with her.

His dad had never remarried, and the sadness Greg III often saw in his eyes pained him deeply. But, then again, what woman could live under the same roof with Elsie Louise Allen. In her mind, no woman was good enough for her only son, and her son could never measure up to the broken dreams she'd had for him to become a powerful politician. Even her son's great success in the worldwide manufacturing industry, and Greg III's rapid climb up the corporate ladder, fell well short of her nagging expectations. And she was quick to share her rancor with anyone within earshot.

"If he hadn't snuck off and married that li'l hussy in college, your daddy would surely be a South Carolina State Senator by now and on his way to making a bid for the White House," Elsie often said in Greg III's presence. Notwithstanding, she'd never laid eyes on the *li'l hussy* she obviously hated so much—who just happened to be Greg III's mother—who'd died giving birth to him. But all Elsie Allen could see was that she would've backed her son all the way to the White House; and, in her mind, anyone she would've backed would be a sure-fire winner.

By choosing to live in the cottage, Greg III was no longer under his grandmother's constant scrutiny. Gone were the days when she could force him to wear dorky blue blazers and bookworm glasses; but, nonetheless, her long tentacles of disapproval found ways to lash out at him.

"Greg III, why are you sitting back there in that drab old cottage?" his grandmother said over the phone. "Come up here to the big house, and let's get together a game of mahjong—"

"Not now, Grandmother Elsie," Greg III replied, struggling to sound polite. "I'm headed out to meet my crew—"

"But you're always hanging out with that bunch of losers, Greg III. You need to find yourself a higher class of friends." Elsie Allen stiffened her back in her favorite chair. "You're going to be company president someday, and then CEO, and those three will still be wallowing around in the dirt—"

"Whatever you say, Grandmother." Greg III reseated his stylish eyewear and clicked off the line. *Wonder what my grandfather ever saw in that old hag? Surely, it was the lines, wrinkles, and that bad attitude that sent him to an early grave!* But as much as he hated it, Greg III stayed close to home so he could keep his finger on the pulse of his daddy's plans. The strain of years of hard work; the trials of being a single parent; and having to deal with a cantankerous old mother had taken its toll on his dad. His health was beginning to fail, and he was looking forward to turning the reins of his empire over to his only son.

Greg III knew that what he was up to with the 4-Gs and the WNL was diametrically opposed to the core values of Allen Textile Mills, Inc. But he'd never quite understood why his dad had taken such a hard-nosed stand to promote racial and gender equality within the company because the company's founder, Greg, Sr., certainly never did. However, Greg III was satisfied to bide his time and change the core values to those of his own liking when he became CEO. *Coddling these blacks and wetbacks, my grandfather must be turning over in his grave! But when I take over, I'll rip these silly rules to shreds and make this the all-white company it was intended to be!*

In the meantime, his grandfather, Greg, Sr., had left him a sizeable inheritance that became available to him when he'd turned 21. Now Greg III was willing to use all of his resources to advance the WNL's cause and get his 4-G buddy, Gus McVey, elected as the new sheriff. He knew he'd be able to double his fortune whenever he took over his daddy's spot as CEO of Allen Textile Mills, Inc.

****

"I know what I'm putting on the line," Greg III said after some serious consideration.

"What?" His three comrades rallied around him with great expectation.

"My family name…that's a given." Greg III ran a nervy hand through his black hair and squinted his cloudy blue eyes. "But I'm also willing to bankroll this entire operation to kick out that clown, Jackson, and elect our buddy…our fellow comrade-in-arms of the White Nationalist League…and the next Sheriff of Nolan County…Gus McVey!"

"Good for you!" They all raised the white-power hand sign and pounded Greg III's back with the requisite number of man-claps. "We knew you'd come through, brother. We knew you wouldn't let us down!"

"We'll lay out our plans to our local WNL unit." Gus salivated. "And boys, if we can pull this off, it'll double our chances to finally get to meet the Grand Master up at the main compound…somewhere deep in these ole woods."

"Yessss!" They all pumped fists in the shadows of their secluded spot. "White Power!"

The tables had finally turned. The 4-Gs were in the driver's seat now. It was their turn to be the superheroes—*Preacher Man*; *Radio Man*; *Money Man*; and *Law Man*—ready and willing to kick butt on behalf of all the white folk of Nolan County—whether they knew it or not. *Now, take that, all you whiny jocks, snarly pretty girls, and worthless half-breeds from good-ole Screamer High!*

CHAPTER 5

Chief Deputy Gus McVey was keeping a cheesy grin in Sheriff Jackson's face by day and plotting his demise with the 4-G Crew by night. Whether on a stake-out or on regular rounds, Gus could be heard giving Sheriff Jackson the highest praise. When any of the other ten deputies—all of which were white with the exception of one, Assa Leckie—would cast any disparaging remarks toward the Sheriff, Gus would always stand-up in his defense. And, when he was in earshot, he was even heard to call Sheriff Jackson, "Boss." In fact, Gus thought he'd bamboozled all of the deputies in the Nolan County Sheriff's Department into thinking he was Sheriff Jackson's biggest supporter.

"Brown-noser!" Deputy Jack Nelson spat his tobacco juice into a paper cup.

"Yeah!" All the other deputies in the locker room nodded their agreement, but they also knew Deputy Nelson had been bitten by the green-eyed monster of jealousy. Nelson had been former Sheriff Magpie's right-hand man; but, now, Gus McVey had beaten him out for the spot with Sheriff Jackson, and he didn't like it one little bit.

Deputy Assa Leckie faked a nod with the rest of the officers. Since Jackson's recent rise to power, he had become the lone token deputy, chosen only to comply with the state's community policing standards. But Assa was Geechee-born and Gullah-raised in the Lowcountry region of South Carolina off the Beaufort Sea Islands, and he was nobody's fool. In addition to his fondness for rice and his Gullah dialect, the midwife had told his mother that he was born with a third eye. He was an only child; never knew his daddy. Given his special gift, however, he was able to see into the hearts of his fellow officers, including that of Chief Deputy Gus McVey, whom he trusted least of all.

Assa had been assigned to partner with Gus in The Presidents a number of times, and he didn't like what he saw. Gus wanted to crack skulls first and ask questions later. On more than one occasion, Assa had issued Gus a stern reminder. "The taxpayers only pay us to apprehend the suspects, mon, not for us to act as their judge, jury, and executioner. That not be our job." Despite Assa's vigilance, however, things were going pretty much according to the 4-G's plan until things took a dark turn.

"Chief Deputy McVey here…ten-four!" Gus issued a snappy response to the emergency call that squawked over his radio.

"Chief Deputy…Gus…you might wanna come on over here, mon." Deputy Assa Leckie's voice trumpeted.

"Over where?" Gus shot back.

"Over here," Deputy Leckie said, reciting the address in his clearest Geechee voice.

"But—" Gus' voice hollowed. "That's my mom's address."

"Yes, sir, it be that," the deputy confirmed. He had little regard for McVey but a total regard for the sanctity of family.

Gus arrived at his mother's home, sirens blazing, only to find the EMTs rolling her body out of her long-time residence on a stretcher. Her frail form was completely covered under a white sheet. "Stop!" Gus said, and the EMTs obliged. With a shaky hand, Gus pulled back the sheet from his mother's stone-cold face. It was badly misshapen, and Gus shot an acid glance at the head technician.

"Most likely, it was a stroke." The technician nodded. "A bad one."

"But…how?" Gus cast a sagging glance at the young, black deputy. "How did you know?"

"Her neighbor across the street called the station when she did not answer the phone or the door," Deputy Leckie said.

"Oh—" Gus breathed, running his hand through his tussled blonde hair and daring the tears to fall from his foggy brown eyes.

"Can we take her, now?" the EMTs said. "We've got to get her to the morgue so the medical examiner can do an autopsy."

"Is that necessary?" Gus asked, already knowing the answer in cases like this when the deceased passed away alone at home.

"Yes, sir, afraid so," the EMT said while rolling her toward the ambulance.

"Is there anything we can do—"

"No!" Gus waved off the other officers and the gathering crowd of looky-loos, and he took long, solemn strides toward the house. He walked into his mother's bedroom and stopped cold in his tracks. The imprint of her body was still lying there under the covers. He took a few more steps into the room and collapsed onto her vanity chair. When he turned and saw his haggard face in the mirror, he almost didn't recognize himself. This was the spot from which his drunken mother had smeared lipstick on her lips and rouge on her cheeks to ready herself for her *company*. This was the spot from which his mother had scolded him so many times for rambling through her drawers.

"Quit pawing through my things!" His mother would smart. "Whatever's in there is none of your business, you li'l snot!"

Well, unfortunately, it was all his business, now. He had no idea what provisions she'd made. *Does she have a will? Does she have a life insurance policy tucked away for her burial expenses? Or is everything gonna fall on me?* Gus had never had a good relationship with his mother, and this was all too sudden for him to take in.

Barring any other recourse, Gus opened one drawer in her dresser and then another. There were papers and letters, none of which could help him, now. When he got to the last drawer though, it was stuck. Something was caught in the back of it that wouldn't allow it to open. Gus tugged and tugged, and then he pulled the dresser away from the wall and pushed. Finally, the drawer gave way at his persistence.

Taped to the very back of the drawer was an envelope, and that's what had gotten stuck. Gus opened it, hoping to find something that would help him handle his mother's sudden death and her final expenses. But, instead, the envelope contained a lone picture of a man—a white man. He was a stocky white guy, mid- to late-thirties, blonde hair, brown eyes, and a thin mustache over thick lips that were set into a satisfied smirk. The man was standing in front of what looked like a church that had a floor-to-ceiling window; the window was adorned with a brilliant, stained-glass cross.

"A white man," Gus mumbled, "I guess it's a far cry better than that other picture I found…of that black mutt." *I wonder who he is? Why did she have his picture hidden in the drawer? Could this man…this white man…could he possibly be…my daddy?*

As it turned out, Gus did have to scrape up his own money for his mother's funeral. Since it didn't much matter, he decided to do it on the cheap. He had his mother cremated, and he scattered her ashes in the alley behind Billy's Biker Bar. *Since this is the place you loved during my childhood…way more than you ever loved me.*

To satisfy the 4-G Crew, however, Gus held a memorial service for his mother in a small chapel provided to him by his buddy, Assistant Pastor Gabe Ingram, at The Church of the Evangelicals. Very few people attended. Sheriff Jackson and some of the deputies passed through to show their respects. Even the WNL dispatched the top aide to the Grand Master to pay their respects. No one was the wiser, but Gus felt very proud to have received such an honor. And, of course, the 4-G Crew was back together again—Gus, Gabe, Greene and Greg III—lifelong friends who'd supported each other through thick and thin, even if the rest of the town barely knew or cared they even existed.

After the services, Gus McVey, looking lean and buff in his departmental-issued, dress blue uniform, cornered his buddy. "Gabe, can I talk to you a minute?" He removed his service cap and smoothed down his blonde hair.

"Of course," Assistant Pastor Gabe Ingram replied. They gave their fond farewells to Greene and Greg III and retired to the preacher's office to talk.

"Here!" Gus slapped down the picture of the white guy he'd found hidden in his mother's dresser drawer.

"Who's that?" Gabe frowned.

"That's what I wanna know!" Gus' thick lips stiffened.

"What?" Gabe shrugged. "I don't get it?"

"You remember that time I found that picture…that black…in my mother's drawer?"

"Yeah, you showed me—"

"Well, I found this one when I was going through her things," Gus said. "But this one was really hidden…in an envelope in the very back of her bottom drawer—"

"And—"

"And I need to know who he is—"

"Why? Why is that so important to you—"

"Important to me!" Gus nearly shouted. "It should be important to us all…you, Greene and me. We don't have a clue who our daddies are. We don't have a clue!" He plopped down into one of the desk chairs.

"Why is that so important to you, Gus?"

"Why? You ask me, why? Because knowing who your daddy is makes all the difference in who you are…as a person…as a man…as a white man. Don't you even listen to what we talk about at our WNL meetings. Knowing you are a full-bloodied white man is so important!"

"Ok-ay," Gabe said, trying to diffuse his friend's hysteria. "Granted, it would be nice to know, but we're adults, now. Is it critical?"

"It is to me," Gus snapped. "You weren't the guy that found a black man's picture squirreled away in your mom's things. What if that…that…inferior…is my daddy…and not this white guy?"

"But what if neither one of them is your daddy, Gus? What difference could it possibly make?"

"It makes all the difference in the world!" Gus' jaws clenched. "And I'm determined to find out once and for all. I won't be able to look at myself in the mirror or any of the other WNL members straight in the eye, not until I know."

"So…what're you planning to do?"

"You've heard of all these online sites where you can get your DNA tested?"

"Yes."

"Then I'm gonna send in my DNA and have it tested," Gus said. If it comes back that I'm anything but white…I think I'll shoot myself in the head with my service revolver—"

"Stop talking nonsense, Gus." Gabe slapped his desk. "Cut it out!"

"Well, for sure I'll drop out of the WNL…and maybe even the Sheriff's Office—"

"One thing at a time." Gabe sagged. "I guess it wouldn't hurt for you to get your DNA tested. You've been wrestling with this for a very long time—"

"All my life…haven't you?"

"Not exactly—"

"But I want you to do it, too," Gus said. "In fact, I want all of us to get it done. We're all in this thing together, right? All-for-one-and-one-for-all, right?"

"Calm down, Gus," Gabe said in his practiced, *I-must-be-talking-to-a-lunatic*, pastoral voice. "Let's just take this one step at a time. If it'll set your mind at ease, yes, I'm willing to go along with you—"

"Do you think Greene and Greg III will, too—"

"I can't speak for them, but you can certainly ask them."

"Thanks, Gabe." Gus breathed a sigh of relief. "You don't know how much better I feel. Thank you, man. I really do need to get this off my chest once and for all!"

CHAPTER 6

Meanwhile, across the tracks, Lucille Jackson had cornered her husband in a heart-to-heart meeting as well. It was nearly a combat zone in the master bedroom of their ranch-style home, located on Ann Street and 5th Avenue, in the better part of Screamer's black community. Since the azaleas had begun to bud, signaling the start of spring, Lucille was thinking it was high time she got started on the rest of her plan to upgrade their social status.

"Bertram, it seems that Nolan County is getting used to having a black sheriff, don't you think?" Lucille started off slowly, sashaying around the bedroom in her black negligee, making sure to cast the best light on her lovely face. What she lacked in the hips, she made up for double in the bosom, and she always kept her finer assets front and center to be sure to remind her husband of his good fortune.

"Where're you going with this, Lucille?" Sheriff Jackson said, familiar with his wife's love for playing the angles. "It's been a long, hard day, baby, and I just wanna get a nice hot shower and lay down in our cozy bed."

"But, Bertram-Baby," Lucille said, blocking his progress into the bathroom, "I don't get to see you all day long and then again half the night. We need to talk over some things—"

"And you know why you don't see me, Lucille?" Bertram pushed out his words through clenched teeth. "Because I'm busting my butt down at that Sheriff's Office trying to do my job. If it ain't my officers trying to figure out ways to trip me up, it's the citizens coming up with a lot of nonsense and petty complaints—"

"Hon-ey, I'm sure your job is very stressful right now." Lucille removed her silk robe to reveal the matching nightie that put her long, sleek legs on full display. "But at some point, we've got to talk about us." She sat on the side of their four-poster bed and patted the smooth, red silk sheets for her husband to join her.

"Okay, Lucille." Bertram took a seat beside her. "Go ahead; I'm listening."

Lucille made a feeble attempt at massaging one of her husband's massive shoulders as she cooed into his right ear, "Bertram, we really do need to move our membership—"

"What membership—"

"Our church membership." Lucille flashed him the eye for such a naive question. "We need to move it over to The Church of the Evangelicals—"

"What are you saying, Lucille?" The long lines deepened in the sheriff's dark brow. "Why on earth would we do a thing like that? We've been at Beulah Bible all of our lives."

"You've been a deacon a long time at Beulah Bible, and what's it gotten you?" Lucille faked a pout. "It's time for you to move on and move up to receive the fruit of your labors, and you can do just that over at The Church of the Evangelicals." Lucille pushed back her freshly-styled, blonde-streaked locks and floated her arms around her husband's hard chest. "After all, you're a big man in this town, now," she said. "You're the Sheriff of Nolan County, Bertram, and they know better than to push you around—"

"Or you—"

"Well, of course," Lucille fished for just the right words, "it goes without saying...whatever benefits you will ultimately benefit me."

"And how will Pastor Renfrow feel about us just up and leaving Beulah Bible because, according to you, it was in large part due to his efforts that I even got elected—"

"That may be all well and good, but Pastor Renfrow has got to understand...along with the other knot-heads in this town...that him and that church have to share you with the larger community—"

"You mean, the white community—"

"Well, certainly!" Lucille flung her arms in exasperation. "Ain't no white folk gonna come stepping-up into Beulah Bible…but you can take the initiative to reach your hands across the tracks to show that you're a man for all the people of Nolan County. That'll go a long way when it's time for your re-election in two years. Did you ever think about that?"

"I've got too much on my plate right now to give that much thought—"

"And neither should you, Bertram-Baby." Lucille pulled in closer to her husband and kissed his strong cheek. "That's my job."

"But what makes you think those white folks will want us at their church?"

"It's a church, ain't it? Well, if they believe God condones racial bigotry, especially in His own church, then they haven't been reading their Bibles. Sha! If they don't believe God loves all His people in the exact same way, they ain't even real Christians—"

"Uh-huh—"

"And, besides, I probably have a lot to offer the women at that white church." Lucille stood to admire herself in the full-length mirror. "If nothing else, I'll bring a different perspective; a different style; a different flavor than they've ever been exposed to…and I can be an ambassador." Lucille glossed her shiny fingertips. "They need to know what's happening down here in The Presidents. Their outreach ministry should be willing to serve the needy anywhere…and especially those close to home—"

"So cut to the chase, Lucille," Sheriff Jackson said, massaging his weary temples. "What're you planning to do?"

"First of all, I've scheduled a lunch meeting next week with Betsy Pritchard, the senior pastor's wife, to discuss your future role at their church…just to test the waters—"

"And if I say, yes, can I go in there, get my shower, and get into this good ole warm bed?"

"Of course, honey," Lucille chirped.

"Then, go; talk to the lady; but don't you dare…under any circumstances…commit me to anything, Lucille…not until you've talked to me first."

"Deal!" Lucille whooped and danced the shimmy-shimmy in front of the full-length mirror while the weary sheriff drug his tired carcass into the shower.

****

As it turns out, earlier that same afternoon, the senior pastor's wife, Betsy Pritchard, had also been having a heart-to-heart with her beloved daughter, Molly. They shared an intimate high tea on the enclosed sunporch, right off of her sprawling veranda. As the daffodils along the walkway swayed in the slow, southern spring breeze, the two of them had enjoyed the bright sunshine and improving temperatures.

Molly Anne Pritchard Ingram dearly loved her mother because she didn't know what her life would've been like if she hadn't been adopted by her and Senior Pastor Pritchard. She knew it was a popular notion, but Molly had never desired to find or connect with her birth mother. She was grateful for the life the Lord had given her with the Pritchards, and she figured it was best to leave well enough alone.

"Thank you, Maude," Betsy Pritchard said as the maid deposited an enameled serving tray of Earl Grey tea, assorted finger sandwiches, and her prized blueberry scones onto the carefully appointed table. The pink-and-white place settings of fine bone china were delicately and tastefully displayed.

"Is there anything else, Miss Betsy," the white-aproned maid replied.

"No, Maude, everything is just lovely," the petite pastor's wife said, granting her a sweet smile.

As she poured their tea, Betsy plummeted her daughter with a steady stream of church and local community gossip. “Did you know Zoe Morgan’s daughter has run off to get married to God knows who in God knows where?” Betsy whispered. “And Zoe is in such a state. We’ve all gathered around her in prayer, but—”

While her mother prattled on, Molly couldn’t help but fondly remember her own wedding ceremony that had been a long time in coming.

****

Gabe and Molly had ultimately agreed to her daddy’s plan. Senior Pastor Mike Pritchard had said they needed to focus on their education before marriage, and that’s what they did. Gabe went off to school at Christwell Bible Seminary in Norfolk, Virginia; and Molly stayed closer to home at Durham Christian College, a small, private college in North Carolina. The couple counted the days between holidays and vacations to be with each other. Gabe also made trips in between on the Greyhound Bus to visit Molly at her school, since neither of them could afford a car.

When Molly first arrived on her campus, some of the students—both male and female—had visibly flinched when she’d flashed them with her startling eyes. On her first trip to the bookstore, the boy behind the counter jumped back from her and shouted, “Whoa! What’s up with you?!? Back home in Screamer, everyone in her close-knit circle had grown accustomed to her mismatched eyes. So, needless to say, it was highly unsettling for Molly to be away from home for the first time—alone, among total strangers—and in a brand-new environment. Nevertheless, she was determined to persevere. She’d convinced herself that the painful adjustment to the hurtful stares and tactless comments was a small price to pay to reach her personal goals. Besides, these strangers didn’t know her, and they didn't owe her anything. *With the help of the Lord, this is my cross to bear.*

Seeing her vulnerability, however, some of the upperclassmen boys thought she'd be ripe for the picking; she was the cute newbie with the unusual appearance. Not realizing that Molly's faith had already helped her come to terms with her abnormality, they figured she'd be willing to do anything they asked to gain their favor and to try to fit in. To that end, one of the brasher sort stepped to her during the first week of class with just such an idea.

"We're having a rush party over at Gamma Tau, and we've been noticing you're here all by your lonesome," one of the frat boys said with a sly grin. "And a bunch of us guys are willing to fix that for you tonight—"

"Oh, I don't know?" Molly held his gaze with her strobing eyes, attempting to decipher his double meaning.

"You might as well be our mascot," the boy said in a nasty whisper. "Look at you…li'l country bumpkin with those spooky eyes…surely, none of the other guys on campus will *ever* want you—"

"Hold up, there!" Molly stopped the boy dead in his tracks to the delight of the students passing by. It was her way to be very direct; she never saw the value of being coy. "Yes, I am from Screamer, South Carolina, but we've got better manners down there than to be downright rude," she said, standing her ground. "The Lord made me sweet, smart and sassy." She flashed her bi-colored eyes on him like halogen high beams and flipped her kinky, blonde ponytail. "And you might not see my worth just by looking at me, but I've got a boy back home who loves me just the way I am…*spooky eyes* and all. Matter of fact, we're engaged to be married. So…you know what you can do with your li'l stupid frat party?" Molly turned on her heels for all the students to see the flounce of her plaid skirt and the beauty of her toned legs marching away. "Stuff it!"

From that time on, the eager boys at Durham Christian College gave Molly a wide berth, and even the popular girls admired her for taking a stand and staying true to her man. And as time went on, Gabe and Molly realized, more and more, that they were totally committed to each other. Although some of their holiday and weekend visits got a little hot and heavy, they'd also maintained their promise to themselves and to her parents to wait for sex until marriage. So, needless to say, on their wedding day, they were anxious to ditch their guests and head off to the Screamer Inn to consummate their marriage vows.

The couple had exchanged their vows in one of the small chapels at The Church of the Evangelicals. Molly wore a simple, long flowing white dress with glittering butterflies at her waist. She swooped her blonde waves into an upsweep with a white bow, no veil. Red-headed Gabe was handsome in his dark suit and red tie. Molly's mother served as her Matron of Honor and her very proud daddy walked her down the aisle into the long-awaited arms of the love of her life. Their vows were simple—to love, to honor, to cherish, in sickness and in health—until parted by death.

This time, Gabe had saved up to buy a single carat diamond to place on Molly's finger, and he was surprised to learn she'd done the same. And at the proper time, Molly placed a simple gold band on her husband's ring finger. There was punch and cake in the fellowship hall, and a serene-looking woman was strumming a harp. That was it. And after a respectable interval, Mr. and Mrs. Gabe Ingram dashed away to spend their first night together as man and wife. And they both agreed it was well worth the wait. *Oh, what a night!*

***

Molly tuned back into her mother's jabbering just as Betsy was saying, "And did you know Rosemary King is expecting a baby?!?"

"Little Rosemary from our church?" Molly went along with her excitement. "I thought she was still in high school."

"No, she graduated last year." Betsy pursed her lips. "Slipped off and got married at the Justice of the Peace the next day. Her mother was so disappointed because they had saved up for a big wedding for their only daughter." She brightened. "But, now, she's expecting."

"I envy her," Molly said. "I really do."

"Huh?" Her mother gaped. "Why do you say that?"

"Gabe and I've been married a year, now, and we're not expecting."

"Oh, I didn't know—" Betsy's breath caught in her throat. "I didn't know you'd be trying to have a baby so soon—"

"It's not so soon, Mommy." Molly giggled. "Gabe and I waited four years to get married, and, now, we're ready—"

"Oh, what I meant was…I thought you were enjoying teaching the young ones so much that you wouldn't want to break away and take a hiatus to have your own child."

"Both Gabe and I want children, Mommy. I thought you knew that." Molly's puzzled eyes spun like a kaleidoscope. "And it's only natural, now, that we're married—"

"And you're not taking…any birth control measures," her mother asked quietly.

"No, Mommy." Molly blushed. "We want to get pregnant as soon as possible."

"But I thought with your careers and all just getting started…I mean…and you both loving children the way you do…I thought you might consider adopting—"

"Adopting!?!" Molly nearly shouted.

"Yes." Betsy flushed. "There are so many unwanted babies out here…babies their mothers don't want or can't afford and—"

"Mommy," Molly said gently, "I know you spent a lot of valuable time working at the clinic with women like that; and I know all the Right-to-Life work you did is near and dear to your heart.

And I know you wanted children of your own that you couldn't have; and I know that's why you and Daddy adopted me. But that's not me and Gabe." Molly's mismatched eyes caught fire with the richness of love she felt for her husband. "Gabe and I are perfectly able to have babies…lots of babies…and that's what we plan to do—"

"Lots of babies—" Betsy's shock registered in her pale blue eyes. "Oh…I didn't know—"

From that anxious moment, until their tea-time ended, Betsy Pritchard never heard another word that her daughter—her adopted daughter—had to say. She had drifted back to an earlier time—a time when she'd first met Molly's birth mother at the abortion clinic. A time that she'd neither told Molly or her own husband about. A time she'd hoped never to have to revisit. But if Molly and Gabe were planning to have babies—*lots of babies*—maybe the time had come that she could no longer avoid. *Oh, my Lord! What have I done?*

CHAPTER 7

It was a perfect spring day for working deals. Lucille Jackson had invited Betsy Pritchard, the senior pastor's wife, to dine with her at The Little Dixie House on Screamer's Town Square. They specialized in fried green tomatoes and meatloaf, and the lunch crowd was tame enough for them to hear themselves talk.

"Hello, Mrs. Prichard," Lucille greeted warmly. She was sporting a floral suit with matching sling-backs, and her blonde streaks were working a halo effect around her lovely face. "So good of you to meet with me today." Lucille fluttered her artfully arched brows and bought eyelashes. She was on her best behavior, and she wanted to be sure to use proper English, which she was perfectly capable of doing when the mood suited her. After all, she was a proud graduate of South Carolina Christian College. *Hmph!*

"My pleasure," Betsy said. She was a plain white woman with mousy brown hair and gentle blue eyes, and she bobbled into her seat with no earthly idea of what to expect. She placed her purse in her lap and took that awkward moment to smooth out the red-and-white gingham oilcloth covering their table.

"This is so nice," Lucille said, fumbling for pleasantries until the sassy waitress came and went. Without asking, she'd plunked down a couple of sweet teas on their table, but Lucille quickly put her in her place. "Seeing as how you didn't ask us what we preferred to drink," she said, "go fetch us some ice water as well." Having squared away that little piece of business, Lucille got down to the serious matters at hand. "Mrs. Pritchard, I don't know if you know it or not, but my husband, Sheriff Jackson, has been a deacon at Beulah Bible for nearly half his life—"

"Is that right—"

"And I was saying to Bertram just the other night," Lucille buzzed as though she were confiding a closely-held secret, "Bertram, now that you're Sheriff of Nolan County, you should expand your borders so that you can serve *all* the people."

"Is that right?"

"We can't just stay down here in The Presidents; you know—"

"Oh, I see—"

"Yes, and I was thinking we could best expand our borders…you know…like in the Jabez prayer…by moving our membership to The Church of the Evangelicals—"

"Our church?" Betsy fumbled her fork back onto her plate and attempted to mask her shock under her white paper napkin.

"Yes." Lucille waited.

"You're considering joining our church?" Betsy restated.

"Yes, we surely are," Lucille said joyfully, "but only if Bertram can hold an office befitting his important station as Sheriff of Nolan County…*a man for all the people*," she said, eagerly recapitulating the newspaper headlines.

"Of course, that's something you'd both have to seriously consider before giving up his current senior post at Beulah Bible," Betsy said, attempting to mask her growing irritation.

"Of course." Lucille took a bite of her meatloaf and reloaded. "But it's also something we'd only consider if your husband has a place for my Bertram on his leadership team—"

"Well, I wouldn't know anything about that." Betsy released a light chuckle. "I'm only a wife; you know."

"I know." Lucille's voice turned up the heat. "And so am I, but I think if our husbands had an opportunity to sit down and discuss it, it might be a win-win for everyone involved…not the least of which, *all* the citizens of Nolan County."

"Well, I guess I could run your suggestion—"

"Request—"

"Well…I could run your request by Senior Pastor Pritchard and let the menfolk take it from there." Betsy sipped her sweet tea with eyes glued on Lucille. She was learning it was best not to let her guard down around this scheming black woman.

"Well, that's as much as I could expect," Lucille said, her voice melting like molten sugar. "Dessert?"

"Oh, but I shouldn't." Betsy chuckled and patted her growing middle, delighted the interrogation was apparently over.

"I don't come here often." Lucille cast a disdainful side-eye toward the Aunt Jemima motif etched on the front window of the establishment. "But I hear tell they prepare a lovely, warm peach cobbler served with *ice-cold* vanilla ice cream." *Hmph...cold and white...just like you!*

****

Chief Deputy Gus McVey and Assistant Pastor Gabe Ingram also had a clandestine meeting of sorts that afternoon out at Nolan State Park, near the spot where Sheriff Jackson had saved the little blonde-haired toddler. It was a warm spring day; kites were flying in the distant breeze, and ducks were gliding on Nolan Lake. The two friends didn't get out of their cars. They parked driver-side-window to driver-side-window so they could speak in the strictest confidence.

"I brought you a sandwich, Gus," Gabe said, offering it out of his window. "Want it?"

"No." Gus brushed the hamburger aside. "Not hungry—"

"What's with you?" Gabe was beginning to get a little agitated. "You brought me all the way out here at lunchtime—"

"I've handled my dead mama's affairs; and, now, it's high-time I get to know—"

"Get to know what, Gus?" Gabe took a healthy bite of his burger. "Make sense—"

"I've gotta know which one of those men in the pictures are my daddy…the white one…or, God forbid, the black one—"

"Oh, you're at that again—"

"Again?!? There is no again!" Gus blasted. "This will haunt me until I have the answer. And I can't move forward with what we're planning until I know."

"So…what will you do, my son?" Gabe teased, using his richest counseling voice.

"I've already done it—"

"What?"

"I told you I would get one of those DNA kits, and I did," Gus said. "I got it from Heritage.com. That site can also help us build our entire genealogy—"

"Then, you went through with it, huh?"

"Of course, I did," Gus said with a snarly smirk. "I'm a man of my word—"

"Okay-okay—"

"And…I got one for all four of us." Gus held up the DNA kits that were tucked away in a discreet brown paper bag.

"You did what?"

"Well, I knew my 4-G Crew wouldn't let me down and leave me hanging."

"Well—"

"One-for-all-and-all-for-one!" Gus recited their unwritten motto. "Right?"

"Right, man." Gabe took a hearty bite of his burger. "If it'll put your mind at ease, I'm sure we're all in."

"Good," Gus said and handed his buddy one of the kits. "Get this done right away—"

"Well, I'll see what I can do." Gabe shrugged. "And the others?"

"I'll give Greene and Greg III their kits, don't you worry—"

"And about that other thing," Gabe said, swiftly changing the subject.

"Oh, you mean our plans with the WNL?" Gus' keen eyes quickly scanned the area to be sure no one could overhear.

"Yup, that's why we're here, right?"

"I spoke privately with our unit prez—"

"I know…Clive Brun—"

"No last names—"

"Oh, that's right—" Gabe covered his slip with two fingers. "But you do know, Clive joined The Church of the Evangelicals—"

"No, I didn't know—"

"Something you ought to consider, too, Gus—"

"Let's not go there, again." Gus grimaced. "I don't think I'm…church material—"

"But—"

"But, anyhoo," Gus said, recovering quickly, "I spoke to Clive about putting our plan on the next meeting agenda—"

"And—"

"And he said," Gus whispered excitedly, "that he'd better not put it on the meeting agenda for all the guys to hear." Gus rescanned their surroundings. "He said that our plan is so wild and radical that he'd better run it by the Grand Master first!"

"What?" Gabe set his burger aside. "Really?"

"And he also said that since our plan revolves around just the four of us…me, you, Greene and Greg III…it might be best if the other guys in the unit don't know about it because they might get too excited; push to get involved; and end up messing up the whole thing—"

"He might be right." Gabe nodded. "Because what we're planning will take precision and subtlety. We don't need any half-cocked cowboys coming in with guns blazing a drawing too much attention to our operation—"

"For sure!" Gus nodded. "That's the same thing the unit prez said. This may be something best kept amongst the four of us until it's done, and then we can all celebrate together!"

"Wow!"

"And I told Clive to tell the Grand Master that when we pull this off, we expect to get a chance to meet him and to get moved up in the organization. 'To the victors go the spoils!'" Gus pumped his fists. "Right?"

"Right—"

"And when the 4-Gs pull this off, we'll finally make our mark…we'll finally fit in—" Gus' voice fogged over from his years of feeling like an outcast.

"So…it's all good…it's just wait-and-see…right?" Gabe said, attempting to snap his friend out of his funk.

"Yup, wait-and-see…*and*…get your DNA test done right away." Gus rallied. "I'll give Greene and Greg III their DNA kits and bring them up to speed on our plans—"

"What's the urgency on the DNA, Gus?"

"I need to know my family's story!" Gus hammered. "And if that black turns out to be my daddy, I'm dropping out of the WNL…and I just might poke my service revolver in my mouth for the last time—"

"Gus—"

"Just get it done, Gabe!" Gus cranked up his chief deputy's vehicle and slung rocks as he peeled away.

CHAPTER 8

Growing up on a little dirt farm in the hills of North Carolina, Betsy Pritchard had always dreamed of living in the lap of luxury. Now, as she peered behind the heavily-draped windows in her stylish French Provincial living room, everyone would say she'd done very well for herself. But Betsy's eyes lingered long out on the sun-streaked veranda, near the spot where she and Molly had shared their quiet high-tea a few weeks before. With all of her daughter's talk of babies that day, Betsy couldn't force down the feelings of doom tracing through her gut. Her mind drifted back to a time she'd kept carefully closeted away—a time before her beloved daughter's adoption—a time she'd tried never to recall.

****

It had been nearly 25 years since Betsy Pritchard, as the senior pastor's wife, had joined the Right-to-Life Movement through The Church of the Evangelicals. A female representative from the state capitol in Columbia, South Carolina had come to speak to their Women's Circle about joining the cause. Betsy immediately caught the fever. Being childless herself, she couldn't conceive of any woman not wanting her baby. Of course, the seminar leader explained the circumstances that might force a woman into such a drastic decision. There was poverty, abuse, neglect, health issues, fear, incest, rape, and any number of other reasons.

The seminar leader had been both direct and compassionate in her presentation. She recounted some horrific cases of incest up in the hills of North Carolina. One case in particular was astonishing to all of the ladies. A man's wife and all five of his daughters were pregnant at the same time, and the man was the father of them all. The youngest of the daughters was only ten years old.

"I'm exposing you to the plethora of issues that confront women who are forced to make some hard choices," the presenter said, "because I want you to be clear with what you'll be up against." She turned to the ladies with sad eyes and said, "But there is another present-day phenomenon that is particularly troubling to all of us who are in this struggle to preserve human life. Young women, and in greater percentages, young white women, are using abortion as a form of birth control," the presenter cleared her raspy throat and added quietly, "especially if they think the baby will be of…mixed heritage. And we also find that this practice manifests itself both in the indiscriminate use of the so-called, morning-after pill, as well as, late-term abortions. It's sad to say that many of these young women are terminating their babies simply for their own convenience or as a way of ridding themselves of their responsibility. However, on the other hand, there are some women who deeply regret their actions, and they feel…feel like there's no hope. But they're wrong; there is hope and forgiveness in Jesus Christ. That's why I'm able to be here with you today."

The presenter's final remark raised some eyebrows amongst the Women's Circle. It led some of them to believe that this topic was probably closer to home than she was willing or able to admit. But none of that resonated with Betsy. No matter how heart-wrenching or evil, nothing could convince Betsy Pritchard that any woman should terminate a pregnancy. She'd had five miscarriages herself, and she was eager for a child of her own. So, she, and her merry band of church ladies, launched out to set the record straight and turn the world around.

Betsy and her Women's Circle took turns marching around the Mayfair Clinic, near the outskirts of Screamer, where abortions were performed daily. They handed out Gospel tracts; distributed convicting literature that damned the practice; made personal contacts; even pleaded with the pregnant women who were making the decision to use the services of the clinic. But, in the minds of some, this well-meaning group was making a nuisance of themselves, and they wanted them to cease their daily protests and quit pestering their prospective clients.

It was on one such occasion, when the Women's Circle had been blocking the entrance of the clinic for days on end, that the director stepped out to make a personal appeal to Betsy and her cohorts. "Ladies!" the director yelled to get their attention. "I know you think you're doing good work here, but what you're actually doing is becoming an annoyance. We have a right to be here and to offer services to the women who feel they need them," the director said, firming her stance. "And I have done everything in my power to keep our Board of Directors from calling the authorities on you because you do not have the proper permit to persist in your pickets. So, if you all know what's good for you, you will break this up right now and go home to your husbands and your children before we call the cops!" The director turned on her heels, went back into the clinic, and slammed the door.

"Is that true?" The ladies turned to Betsy, who they'd looked to as the unofficial leader of the group. "Do we have a right to be here?"

Betsy looked dazed. "I really don't know," she said. "I never filed for any kind of permit. Did any of you?"

They all quizzed each other with blank stares.

"Then, I guess we'd better have the church's attorney look into it before we all find ourselves in the slammer." Betsy's attempt at humor fell as flat as an overdone souffle, and the disgruntled women began to disperse.

However, as Betsy rounded the corner to her car, she came upon a young woman sobbing against a white oak tree. As was her nature, Betsy couldn't resist reaching out to the poor creature. "Is there anything I can do to help you?" Betsy offered. Little did she know, in that very moment, she was on a collision course with her own destiny.

The young woman was startled, and she tensed, shaking her head.

"Can I ask what's the matter?" Betsy persisted in a quiet tone.

"I…I don't want to go in there." The young woman nodded toward the clinic. "But I must."

"Why must you?" Betsy said sternly. "Destroying life is not God's way."

"God understands!" the young woman clapped back. "But you don't! How could you?" She clasped her arms tightly across her middle. "A woman like you…who has everything…who knows everything. How could you possibly understand?"

"But I—" Betsy gasped, not quite knowing how to counter.

Without another word, the young woman wiped her eyes on her sleeves and proceeded to cross the street to the clinic.

"Don't do it!" Betsy grabbed her arm and slowed her progress. "Please, talk to me. I want to help. I really do want to understand—"

"Can you understand this?" The young woman shook off Betsy's grip. "I was raped!" Her eyes flooded with tears, and she raced across the street to the clinic.

****

Just then the home phone rang, shaking Betsy from the torture of her daydreams. "Hel-lo."

"Mommy!" Molly shouted excitedly, her colorful eyes strobing a galaxy of light. "Guess what! Guess what!"

"Are you alright?" Betsy shuttered.

"Oh, I'm fine. Just fine!" Molly rejoiced. "You remember our conversation over tea the other day?"

"Yes—"

"Well, Gabe and I don't have to wait any longer—"

"What?"

"It's a secret, Mommy…shhhh! I haven't even told Gabe…not yet—"

"What? What?"

"I'm pregnant, Mommy. We're pregnant!" Molly shrieked with joy. "We're pregnant!"

"Oh, no—" Betsy's voice dribbled, and the telephone fell from her trembling hand. *Oh, my God, no!*

CHAPTER 9

For days, all Betsy Pritchard could hear, ping-ponging around in her troubled brain, were her daughter's last words: *"Mommy, I'm pregnant...we're pregnant."* She hadn't been able to eat or sleep since Molly had made her announcement, and her husband was beginning to notice the strain.

"Honey, is there something the matter?" Senior Pastor Mike Pritchard asked his wife.

"No-no, honey…not really—"

"It's not the thing with that Lucille-woman is it?"

"What thing?" Betsy struggled to focus.

"You know…about her wanting me to meet with her husband—"

"Oh, Sheriff Jackson, you mean." Betsy chuckled nervously, looking for any way out. "Well, I don't know, Mike, it could be. That Lucille-creature was very troubling—"

"Well, I don't want you worrying your pretty, little head about that." Her husband reassured her. "I've got it all handled—"

"You do?" Betsy said, happy to refocus the conversation away from her true concerns. "How did you fix it?"

"Well, you see, I had my secretary call his office and set up an appointment with Jackson for next week."

"Oh?"

"Yes, and when we meet, I'll see what he's after—"

"But his wife, Lucille, said he'd never be satisfied with anything less than being on your leadership team—"

"Well, we'll just have to see about that." The pastor bounced his coffee mug back onto the table. "Nobody dictates to me who I put on my leadership team—"

"Well, alright then, dear—" Betsy's response was both sweet and appropriate, but her mind had already drifted back to the time before Molly's adoption—a time she had always hoped she'd never have to discuss with her husband.

****

After the last altercation with the director of the Mayfair Clinic, Betsy and her Women's Circle secured the proper permits through the church's lead attorney to continue their daily pickets. They were faithful to their mission to shut down the abortion clinic. It was at the close of one of their pickets that Betsy had spotted the same woman she'd seen some days before; the one who'd been crying by the white oak tree.

"Hello!" Betsy called. "Can we talk?" The young lady quickened her gait, but Betsy caught up with her and walked alongside. "Have you made your decision yet?"

"Yes." The young lady tensed.

"May I ask what you've decided?" Betsy matched her stride for stride.

"My abortion is scheduled…if you must know…next week—"

"Please, please don't do it," Betsy said. "You'll regret it for the rest of your life—"

"No, I won't!" The girl picked up the pace. "What I'll regret is looking at that cursed baby for the rest of my life!"

"But why?" Betsy said, nearly in tears. She was so tired of trying to convince young girls about the sanctity of life while she, herself, longed so desperately to give birth.

"Because—"

"Why?" Betsy pressed.

"Because…I…I was raped…and I…I can't let my mama…my brother…my family know!" The young girl sobbed uncontrollably, and Betsy shouldered her in a tender embrace.

"It's alright." Betsy soothed the young girl's back. "Everything is going to be alright—"

"No, it's not!" The girl pulled away from her grasp. "That's easy for you to say 'cause you're white—"

"But—"

"Just like that evil white man that raped me!"

"Oh, I didn't know—"

"You…you privileged white folk!" The girl recoiled. "You think you can do anything…to anybody…and just get away with it!"

"You're right." Betsy immediately took up her cause. "What that man did was wrong, and he should be punished to the fullest extent of the law—"

"Ha! Sure!"

"Have you gone to the authorities?"

"No!"

"And why not?"

"Because they're all white like you…the man who raped me was white…and nobody'll do a thing about it—"

"Oh—" Betsy was stunned in her tracks. "Well, I hate to admit it," she said, "but you're probably right. I've never known Sheriff Magpie and his band of crooks to do anything for anybody in this county…especially not a woman—"

"And that goes double for a black woman—"

"So, what're you going to do—"

"I'll get rid of this demon seed…once and for all…and then I'll get on with my life—"

"Which is?"

"I know it's hard for you to believe," the young girl said, "but I'm a sophomore in college at NC A&T…or leastwise I was before all this happened. I was just home for Christmas Break when he raped me. And now it's Spring Break, and I'm forced to come back here to this clinic…before I start to show. And then I can go back to my classes, and nobody'll be the wiser—"

"Except you!" Betsy steamed. "You'll know what you've done, and it will follow you for the rest of your life—"

"Better that than having to explain to this po' baby that its daddy is a rapist—"

"What's your name?"

The young black girl shifted her weight cautiously. "Cora," she finally replied. Her features were strained, but lovely—curly, black natural hair; and somber, mossy brown eyes.

"Well, Cora...I'm Betsy...Betsy Pritchard...and I'm blessed to make your acquaintance."

"Yes, ma'am." Cora straightened her posture and wiped her tears with the backs of her hands.

"When are you due?"

"Probably in the fall—"

"What if—" Betsy seized upon the opportunity. "What if you didn't have the abortion—"

"Then, what'll I tell my boyfriend?" Cora slowly shook her head. "We've been talking about getting married when we graduate—"

"What if," Betsy continued, "what if I were to pay for you to go somewhere very private? Your family could still think you were away at college, and you could tell your boyfriend something that would keep him on hold until you got back—"

"What're you saying?"

"I'm saying, you could go somewhere private and have the baby; and then, go back to your normal routine—"

"But—"

"Just think about it," Betsy said. "You wouldn't have to harm the baby; and, later, you could go back to your normal life, and nobody would ever know—"

"Yeah—" Cora considered her offer. "But what about the baby? What would happen to the baby?"

"Someone could adopt the baby." Betsy was formulating her plan as she spoke. "I...I could adopt the baby—"

"What?" Cora's jaws flapped "You? You? But…you're a white woman—"

"I know…and the baby may look white, too," Betsy said. "I read somewhere that when an interracial couple has a baby, it's more than a 50/50 chance that the first baby will have white features—"

"But…but what if it doesn't—"

"Then…we could put the baby up for adoption, and I'll help some other blessed couple adopt it. I've got a whole network of families at my disposal—"

"But—"

"But either way, Cora," Betsy said, "the baby will still be alive. And that's the important thing here, right…keeping the baby alive?"

"I guess…I guess you're right." Cora felt weak in the knees. "I really…really don't wanna kill my baby—"

"The man that raped you was an unmitigated scoundrel, no doubt, but it's not the baby's fault." Betsy was sobbing now. "It's not the baby's fault! Please, let the baby live—"

"How can you afford to put me up for nearly nine months?" Cora quibbled.

"Well, let's just say…I've got my own resources," Betsy said, referring to the hefty account she'd amassed through her five miscarriages. Each time, she'd saved her money to make sure her baby's life and surroundings were the very best.

"Well, if you can promise…if you can promise me…I won't have to tell my family or let my boyfriend know my whereabouts…I may be willing to see things your way—"

"You have my solemn pledge," Betsy swore on that fateful day. "I'll set you up in a good place where no one can find you; pay all of your expenses; and I will gladly adopt the baby and care for it like it's my very own…if it turns out to be white—"

"And if it turns out to be black—"

"I've got friends who'll adopt it, no problem!" Betsy set her right hand over her heart. "I know lots of women who'd love to have a baby…a baby of any race or color…no questions asked." *Oh, my Lord, thank You for hearing my cries, answering my prayers…and sending me this precious, precious baby!*

CHAPTER 10

As arranged, Senior Pastor Mike Pritchard met with Sheriff Bertram Jackson at his home rather than at The Church of the Evangelicals. He thought they'd both be more comfortable there. There was a tennis court on the grounds, and the preacher was still dressed in his gingham shorts and pink polo after hitting a few balls against the wall for his morning exercise. The sheriff was dressed in his official tan uniform, but since the temperatures were on the rise, he'd opted for the short-sleeved version that put his brown, brawny biceps on full display. A murder of crows could be heard scolding in the distance; and a persistent woodpecker was having its way with a massive, old oak; but the gentle, call-and-response melody from the Carolina wrens nestled nearby provided them with an atmosphere of serenity.

"Thank you, Maude," the pastor said politely as the white-aproned maid set their refreshments under the covered veranda. The black woman snuck a quick peek at the sheriff and nodded her head discreetly. Sheriff Jackson did the same. Of course, he knew the woman and her whole family. They lived across the tracks on 1st Avenue in The Presidents.

"May I offer you some lemonade?" The pastor passed him the silver serving tray, along with a pulpit-practiced smile.

"Don't mind if I do," Sheriff Jackson said and helped himself to one of the tall, cool glasses topped off with a sprig of mint.

"My wife tells me she had lunch with your wife not too far back." The pastor gripped his glass. "Guess the women have been putting their heads together on us, huh?"

"About that," Sheriff Jackson said, "I just want you to know I didn't send my wife on that particular mission."

"Oh, it's alright. It's past time the two of us got together to have a little chat." The pastor stretched out as though he were the king of the castle. "Are you enjoying your new assignment? Are the people of Nolan County treating you well?"

"Well, like everything in life," Sheriff Jackson replied wisely, "there're always a few bumps in the road." He sipped his lemonade. "That's why the Lord put us here…to straighten them out—"

"Well said!" The pastor's voice clapped. "We *are* the keepers of the vineyard—"

"Exactly."

"Well, I can see you've been getting some mighty good teaching over there from Pastor Renfrow at Beulah Bible—"

"Yes, sir," the sheriff said, "Pastor Renfrow does a real good job, and I've been under his leadership my whole life—"

"Which brings me to wonder," the senior pastor said, seizing the opening, "why're you and your wife considering moving your membership to our church?"

"Well, to tell you the truth, we haven't discussed it that much." Sheriff Jackson shifted in his chair and reseated the gun on his right hip. "It's just one of my wife's ideas to be sure I make myself accessible to all the citizens of Nolan County—"

"And not just the ones on your side of town—"

"Exactly."

"Then, what are your thoughts on the matter?" The preacher prodded.

"Well, like I said, I'm open to branching out to make myself more available to all of my constituents, but—"

"But—"

"But I am loyal to Beulah Bible, and I'd hate to leave there just for the sake of sitting in the pews somewhere else…if you know what I mean—"

“I think I know very well what you mean.” Senior Pastor Pritchard raised his brows. “You want to put your God-given gifts to work wherever you attend services—”

“That’s it!” The sheriff sat up straight in his chair. “You’ve got it.”

“Well, to be frank,” the preacher said, but it was far from the truth, “our Deacon Board is at top capacity right now.”

“I see—”

“And I understand you’ve been a deacon at Beulah Bible for many years.” The preacher lowered his eyes and his glass. “But I’m afraid we wouldn’t be able to offer a similar post to a man of your seasoned skills.”

“Oh, I see,” the sheriff said, feeling he was about to get what most black men get who want to move ahead—the big heave-ho.

“But—” The pastor carefully constructed his next sentence. “But I am willing to talk it over with our leadership team and determine if we can find a suitable post for a man of your obvious gifts and talents.” The preacher added a chuckle. “Afterall, a man doesn’t become Sheriff of Nolan County without the Lord…or the people…on his side.”

Sheriff Jackson hadn’t been too keen on moving their membership from Beulah Bible to The Church of the Evangelicals when Lucille had brought him the idea; but now, it was feeling like a challenge from which he could not back down. He took a long sip of his lemonade, replaced the classic Waterford crystal glass squarely onto its matching coaster, and issued the preacher his parting word, “Exactly!”

****

On the other side of town, the 4-G Crew was also having a meeting in the grove of trees on the far end of Nolan Park. This had been their getaway spot since they were kids. The little isolated notch in the woods was near the lake, and it was outfitted with a grill and picnic table. Greene brought enough food to tide them over while their secret pow-wow was in session. They each grabbed a longneck out of the big ice cooler resting on the back of Gus' souped-up pickup. It was their favorite local brand—brewed right there in South Carolina—*Rebel Beer*.

"So…what did our unit prez…Clive…have to say when you laid out our plan to him?" Greene Jones' fat face jiggled eagerly as he gave the T-bones a quick turn on the grill.

"I told you before." Gus McVey scowled; he was still donning his chief deputy's uniform. "Clive thinks it's a go…*and*…he also ran it pass the Grand Master—"

"He did?" Greg III gaped. "What did he say?"

"Slow down, guys," Gabe said, ever the reasoned clergy. "Give Gus a chance to get it all out—"

"Thank you, sir!" Gus nodded at Gabe in jest. "Well, here is where we stand. The Grand Master told Clive that essentially he liked our idea—"

"Alright!"

"The Grand Master said that black church burnings have worked in the past in a number of states to keep these misfits and ingrates in their place. And he agrees that since this mongrel Jackson stole the sheriff's election right from under our noses, we must step-up our efforts to make our power known—"

"Yes!"

"So…let me be clear," Greg III said in his businesslike manner, "we have the green light to burn down the three black churches in Screamer—"

"Well, yeah!" Gus pursed his thick lips and restated the case. "The Grand Master has given the four of us the green light to burn down the three black churches in The Presidents so we can discredit Jackson in the white and black communities—"

"It's a masterful plan when you think about it," Greene said. "All we need to do is get Jackson and the other deputies out of place at the proper time, and then burning down those old tinderboxes will be a breeze—"

"Not so fast!" Gabe raised his hands in objection. "For us to get it done, we've got to act with great precision. The operations will have to go like clockwork. We can't afford to get our hands dirty—"

"Or get caught!" Greene's fat face creased. "I'm a big-time radio personality in this town. We can-not get caught—"

"No, we can't!" Greg III yammered. "My daddy would kill me! The people in this county depend on our mill for their livelihood, and we can't be disgraced! That mill has been in my family for three generations—"

"We know, Greg III! We know!" Gus flamed. "None of us wants to get caught because we can't let anything stop me from becoming sheriff, right?"

"And what did the Grand Master have to say about that?"

"The Grand Master said he'd back me all the way if we can pull this off—"

"And you know what that means!" Greene clinked longnecks with Greg III. "We'll finally get the respect we've always deserved in this town—"

"But—" Gus said, cutting their celebration short, "the Grand Master added one more important thing—"

"What?"

"The Grand Master said, 'This is our op and our op alone,'" Gus recounted. "If we pull off the three church burnings, the WNL will take full credit and breathe the fear of God into these misfits around here. But if we screw it up in any way…*any way*…the WNL will disavow any knowledge of us or our actions, and we'll be kicked out of the WNL in disgrace. Is that clear?"

"Yes." They nodded in concert. "In other words, we're on our own—"

"Indeed!" Gus said. "So, once we get started, we can-not…under any circumstances…foul this up!"

"Or get caught!"

"And nobody can get hurt!" Gabe said, no longer able to hold his peace on that point. "I insist on that. I'm still a minister of the gospel, and I can't condone any loss of life."

"As you say, Preacher Man." They all ambled to the picnic table and took a seat.

"Okay, we'll do it when the churches are empty." Gus snarled. "None of the jigaboos will have to get hurt—"

"If Jackson knew what we were planning, he'd have a stroke!" Greg III snorted.

"True!" Gus cheesed. "But he'd never suspect me as having any part in it. I've got that fool bamboozled—"

"We'll kick out Jackson just like we're gonna kick that spook out the White House!" Greene cheered as he plated their bloody steaks.

"But at least his mama's white—" Greg III dared mention.

"Doesn't matter!" Gus flamed. "Groups all over this country, just like the WNL, won't be satisfied until we've put a purebred Arian brother in that half-breed's place—"

"And get all our rights back!" Greene crammed in a big bite of steak.

"And when we've pulled off these church burnings, we'll most certainly get her done." Gus took a long swig of his beer.

"Everybody in Nolan County will want Jackson's head on a stake when those churches go up in flames! You can count on it!"

"For sure, brother. For sure!"

"But we don't have the luxury of time!" Gus drug them back on point. "We have from now until the last day I can get my name on the ballot."

"That's right—"

"So…we'll start with the first one." Gus assumed full command. "We'll start with that little storefront job just across the tracks. I think they call that one…Holy Ghost Headquarters."

"That's the one!"

"I'll make the plan, and we'll work the plan!" Gus rallied the troops.

"White Power!"

"All-for-one-and-one-for-all!" Gus trumpeted their motto and slammed his prized keychain with the G-initial onto the picnic table. The other three followed suit, slapping down their G-initials in rapid succession, forming a straight line. "Count 'em off!" Gus hooted. "One. Two. Three. Four. We're the 4-G Crew! Nothing can stop us now!" They whooped around the picnic table like four little boys of privilege readying for the warpath. Clanging their longnecks like sabers, they whipped up their emotions to a frenzied pitch. The weather girl at radio station WSCR had been predicting that 2015 would bring a long, hot summer to Screamer, South Carolina, but she didn't know diddly. It was only May, and things were already starting to sizzle!

CHAPTER 11

Like Lucille, Sheriff Jackson was approaching the 50-year mark. Although, in Lucille's case, not another solitary soul on the planet would ever be privy to her exact number of summers. The sheriff, on the other hand, had no such apprehension. He possessed that rugged, tough cop look—hard body, steady gait, square jaw, and greying slightly at the temples—something Lucille had been nudging him to rectify with a little bottle of black hair dye.

"This society is all about youth, Bertram," Lucille informed him as she spritzed her neck with her high-priced perfume. "For you to succeed in this world, you've gotta be sure to look the part; and that means…you've gotta look young.

The Jacksons had no children. Lucille wasn't about to let a baby ruin her svelte figure. Although she had a host of cousins, she was an only child, and she had Bertram fooled that a low birth rate ran in her family. Lucille figured she had passed her baby-having prime, but just to be on the safe side, she continued to secretly take her birth control pills each day.

"So…what did that white preacher have to say for himself?" Lucille started in over dinner.

"You mean, Senior Pastor Pritchard?"

"Yeah, that's what I said, didn't I?"

"Well, it's your idea to go over to that white church, Lucille, so you might as well get used to calling those folk by their rightful names."

"Whatever." Lucille pouted. "But what did the preacher say?"

"We had nice refreshments out on his plush veranda." Bertram chided his wife's impatience. "And then he said…he'll see—"

“He’ll see what?

“He’ll see if he and his lily-white leadership team can locate a suitable place for the likes of a black man like me—”

“And what does that mean?”

“It means he’ll get back with me,” Bertram said. “Besides, we need the time to talk it over with Pastor Renfrow. We owe him that much—”

“If you say so.”

“And, in the meantime, Senior Pastor Pritchard will get back with me and let me know where they stand—”

“You trust him?”

“He has to do it, Lucille.” Sheriff Jackson shrugged. “The man gave me his word—"

“But you know how white folk are, Bertram, when it comes to money and power,” Lucille said. “You can’t trust ‘em as far as you can throw a fat elephant. People of color, we generally want peace, harmony, and equal rights; but white folk want money, position, and power, and they’re willing to do anything to get it. Just ask these Third World Nations; ask the Indians; shucks, ask our own slave ancestors. White folk will sell-out their own mamas if the price is right—”

“Lucille—”

“My daddy trusted ‘em, and what did it get him?” Lucille bobbed her head to make her point. “I’ll tell you what it got him…a bullet in the back o’ the head; that’s what it got him. And just ‘cause that plant boss didn’t like the kind o’ car he was driving—”

“Yes, that was a mighty fine-looking Cadillac—”

“But his plant boss thought it was too good for the likes of a black man.” Lucille’s voice cracked. “And right out there at Allen Textile Mills, too—”

“But the Lord worked it all out, Lucille,” Bertram said, his voice washing over his wife like a sweet caress. “And, baby, that’s all that matters—”

"Black *lives* matter!"

"All lives matter, Lucille." Bertram pushed back from the table. "God made us all—"

"That may be so, but it's black lives that always seem to come under the threat of prejudice, ridicule, and even death. If you'll recall, it took nearly five years before they brought that white man's sorry tail to justice, and that wouldn't have happened if my daddy had been white—"

"But—"

"And that low-down Sheriff Magpie and his wicked gang of thieves, they knew all the time who'd done the murder—"

"But that was nearly 25 years ago, honey; it's all water under the bridge now," her husband said. "If you'll recall, they sent that white man to the electric chair—"

"Eventually!" Lucille broke into a spiteful laugh. "After nearly 20 years on death row."

"Lucille, honey, you sound as disappointed with the state of race relations in Screamer as my sister, Cora—"

"Well, it's good to know that me and your sister can agree on something!"

"And sometimes, Lucille, I think you're a bigger racist than all of these white folks put together—"

"I make no bones about it, Bertram. I do have me a powerful love for black folk. Against all odds, we're beautiful, resilient, and smart, and I wouldn't trade us for anybody on God's green earth." Lucille's voice swelled. "But there is one *big* difference between me and these white racists—"

"And what's that?"

"I may be a racist, but I ain't no murderer!" Lucille teared.

"I hear you, honey, and you're right." Her husband raised his hands in surrender. "Love is what makes the difference. These white racists aren't operating out of a love for their own race…because we're no threat to them. They're acting purely out of their own hatred for us—"

"Us…and anybody that doesn't look like them."

"Yup, racism is their own issue alright. It's like a sickness with those people. It's hard-wired into their DNA." The sheriff shook his head in dismay. "And only the power and love of Jesus Christ can change that—"

"And only if they let Him."

"So…is that the real reason you want us to go up to that white church?" the sheriff asked. "Do you want us to show the kids in The Presidents that at least somebody's making an effort to improve race relations in Screamer?"

"Naw, these kids down here are smarter than that, Bertram," Lucille said in a huff. "They know these white folk ain't never gonna change—"

"Then why—"

"Because the tables have turned, Bertram-Baby, and it's our time to shine!"

"Huh?"

"In spite of all the odds, the President of the United States of America is a black man. And to top that off, I finally got that slimeball Magpie out of office after 25 years." Lucille's eyes glazed over with sheer satisfaction. "White folk never pay us any attention unless we've got something they really, really want…money, land, power…or they need a grinny-grinny black face in one of their crowd scenes. But now that you're the Sheriff of Nolan County, Bertram Jackson, it's their turn to sit up and take notice…whether they like it or not!"

****

On the same evening, Senior Pastor Mike Pritchard was sharing true confessions with Gabe Ingram during a prearranged, closed-door meeting at his church office. He wanted to keep his wife, Betsy, out of earshot. "You're not only my assistant pastor, but my beloved son-in-law as well," the senior pastor said, launching his appeal.

"I'm glad you see it that way." Gabe smiled warmly. "Because I certainly feel the same."

"And that's why I asked you to meet with me here…after hours so to speak—"

"Is there something wrong? Are you alright?"

"I'm fine, just fine." The senior pastor tapped his round belly. "I might be too full in the middle, but I'm trying to work that off on the tennis court."

"Okay." Gabe's red hair glistened under the lamplight. "Then what?"

"I had an interesting lunch today—"

"Oh?" Gabe drew closer to the senior pastor's grand mahogany desk in his lavishly-appointed office. Betsy had outdone herself with the décor. Since she had the church's full coffers at her disposal, she'd spared no expense.

"Yes, it was out there at my house," his father-in-law said. "I had the pleasure of meeting with the new sheriff in town…Sheriff Jackson—"

"Jackson?" Gabe's ears perked, ever eager to keep his 4-G Crew and the WNL well-informed.

"Seems like his wife, Lucille, wrangled the appointment out of Betsy." The senior pastor reared back in his plush ergonomic chair. "You know how sweet and unsuspecting our Betsy can be, and it seems that this Lucille-woman is quite a character—"

"Oh, I see—"

"But, anyway, we had lunch out at the house…Sheriff Jackson and me…and I bet you can't guess what the subject was—"

"Some legal matter…dealing with the church…or one of our wayward parishioners—"

"You'd think." Mike Prichard chuckled. "But it was nothing like that—"

"Then what?"

"Well, it seems like Jackson and his wife want to move their membership up here…to The Church of the Evangelicals—"

"No!" Gabe's mouth gaped.

"Oh, yes," the senior pastor said. "I really think it's all his wife's idea, but Jackson is going along with it—"

"So…what did he want from you…your blessings?"

"No." Mike Pritchard bounced around in his chair. "Can you believe it? He wants my support—"

"Your support…I don't get it?

"Seems he's a senior deacon at Beulah Bible down there in The Presidents, and he doesn't want to join our church without some assurance that he can be a member of our leadership team—"

"You mean he thinks he can just come up here and become a deacon at The Church of the Evangelicals?" Gabe said, letting his racist bent peek from under his clerical collar.

"No…he wasn't quite that pushy." The senior pastor leaned in closer, and the two men put their heads together. "He was more or less fishing for an answer as to what leadership role he might be able to play if he moved up here. And I guess his contemplation is not unreasonable. The man is the Sheriff of Nolan County; you know—"

"Yeah," Gabe spoke without thinking, "but maybe even that'll change soon—"

"Maybe." The senior pastor cleared away the frog in his throat. "But, until then, we've got a black sheriff looking to join our leadership team. What do I tell the man?"

"Have you spoken to any of the deacons?"

"No, not yet. I didn't want to get them all riled up before I had a suitable solution to offer them."

"I see—"

"And just what do you think about it, Gabe? What can we do with Sheriff Bertram Jackson here at our church?"

Gabe had been deep in thought since the conversation had begun. He was noodling for a way this unexpected turn of events could work in favor of the 4-G's plan. "Well, let me think," he said. "We couldn't possibly let Jackson be a deacon—"

"No-no," the senior pastor agreed. "That post is far too visible, and we don't want to get our major tithe-paying members upset."

"Right." Gabe followed along with his train of thought. "But we could contrive an opening on, say…the Trustee Board—"

"Go ahead—"

"In fact, I think we could construct a kind of…Trustee Training Program…with Jackson as our only student…since there's only one vacancy on the Trustee Board…now that old man McIntyre passed away—"

"And-and—"

"And I could drum up a curriculum that'll be so difficult and time-consuming that Jackson will drop the idea on his own," Gabe said. "This would be an intensive program…with lots of numbers, graphs, and financial principles…which could run as long as say, six months…with classes through the week and on the weekends—"

"And then we'll see just how committed Jackson will be about completing the training—"

"There you have it! You can impress upon Jackson that the Chairman of the Trustee Board is none other than the Honorable Greg Allen II, CEO of Allen Textile Mills, Inc., and he's a stickler for keeping a tight ship and doing things just right."

"And, if perchance, he should complete the rigorous training, Jackson will be on the Trustee Board, and that's our least visible ministry—"

"And as a neophyte member, I'm sure Greg II won't ever allow Jackson to get too close to the real money or to the real facts about how our church finances are structured—"

"That's right—"

"And by that time," Gabe spoke out of his intimate knowledge of the 4-G's plan, "Mr. Jackson will no longer be the Sheriff of Nolan County—"

"Think so—"

"With strong assurance." Gabe offered a sly wink.

"And then Bertram and Lucille Jackson will slink back to Beulah Bible where they belong. Because you know how it is, Gabe; you let one of them in, and they'll try to take over—"

"Indeed!"

"Good!" Senior Pastor Mike Pritchard grinned and clasped hands in league with his son-in-law. "I'll alert our leadership team; notify Jackson; and we'll set him up right away…on his road to failure."

CHAPTER 12

"Whoo-hoo!" Gus shouted, nearly jumping out of his own skin. "Guys, I am so relieved! I feel like a big weight's been lifted off my chest—"

"Thanks for letting us in on it, Gus. We're happy for you, too!" The other 4-Gs stroked his ego and plastered his back with the requisite number of man-claps. It was Sunday evening, and they were all hunkered down with their favorite longnecks at their secret meeting spot by Nolan Lake.

"Gus, man, even the deep creases in your forehead are starting to lighten up—"

"Yeah, guys." Gus granted them a rare but genuine smile. "You just don't know. I was scared…real scared. And what with our plans to keep all these misfits in line, I just didn't need all that stress and doubt hanging over my head—"

"We understand." Greg III nodded. "You have been wrangling with this since we were in grade school—"

"True, Greg III, but did *you* get your DNA tested like I asked?" Gus scolded his friend. "No-oo…you did not—"

"But I've been awfully busy—" Greg III stammered.

"But the rest of us did," Gabe said, attempting to ease Greg III off the hook.

"And the results are in…we are all *white* guys!" Gus let out a wild whoop that sent the nearby squirrels scampering for cover.

"And here's our evidence to prove it—" Greene waddled to the picnic table as the other members of the 4-G Crew gathered around to spread out their DNA test results.

"Mine shows Eastern European and Irish," Gabe said.

"That's probably why you're such a carrot-top, huh?" Greene tussled Gabe's red hair.

"Mine shows white guy…through and through!" Gus crowed. "Look at this…Scandinavian, Scottish, and Eastern European." Gus scrubbed his blonde head with a tight fist. "Now all I've got to do is build my family tree. I've got to find out if that white guy in my mom's picture…well…I need to know if that guy's my dad—"

"One step at a time, Gus," Gabe said, cautioning him like a wise counselor. "You've already crossed a major hurdle. The rest will come. You'll find out soon enough, and you'll know once and for all—"

"Greene, I see yours is showing Irish and German." Greg III took a business-like look at their statistics. "Is that why you're such a sausage-hog, *Fat Boy*?"

"He's not *The Fat Boy*…no, not anymore!" Gus jumped to his defense. "Don't you dare call us by the same names those jerks used at Screamer High!"

"I only thought of it," Greg III whined, "because I heard they're planning for our five-year class reunion—"

"We're not going!" Gus stomped, and his work boot sent the red dust flying. "The next time those losers see me, I'll be Sheriff of Nolan County, and they'll be licking my boots."

"You're right!" They all fell in line.

"And don't forget, Greg III, it was Greene…and not you…who manned-up and got his DNA test done—"

"Lighten up, Gus!" Gabe said, tiring of Greg III being treated like the underdog. "It's no big deal. We already know who his daddy is—"

"True." Gus pursed his lips. "Sorry, Greg III, I guess I'm just a little excited to put all this behind me."

"I understand, Gus." Greg III tendered him a weak smile. "And I've been working hard at the mill, too. This operation to get you elected sheriff comes with a pretty hefty price tag, and I'm trying to line myself up to be my daddy's next company president in order to fund our plans—"

"Well, in that case, maybe you do get a pass—"

"Besides, it's not too late for him to get his test done," Gabe said, fulfilling his role as diplomat.

"That's right," Greg III said, "I…I will get it done…I promise…I just need a little more time to square things away at the mill—"

"No prob!" Gus relented. "Besides, now that we all know we've got the right bloodline, we've got bigger fish to fry—"

"So…we're moving forward with our plan—"

"Yup, next week—"

"So soon?"

"There's no time like the present, and we've waited long enough," Gus said. "Besides, we don't want the WNL to think we're getting cold feet—"

"I'm ready!" Greene said. "Just tell me what and when.

"I'm in, too." Gabe shrugged.

"And I'll finance whatever we decide." Greg III committed.

"Well, we're gonna hit that storefront one first…Holy Ghost Headquarters," Gus said. "We'll do it next Monday. That gives us all this week to get ready—"

"Wow!"

"Why next Monday?"

"Because after Sunday night, there's nobody at those churches until maybe Wednesday or Thursday night. And across the tracks, you can roll up the sidewalks after dark. I've made sure of that." Gus chuckled. "I've been patrolling that area hot and heavy for months, and them lackeys know I'll whip some heads if I catch 'em out after dark."

"Smart move—"

"So, *Preacher Man*," Gus said, turning to Gabe, "you know what your job is?"

"Yes!" Gabe soldiered at attention. "Bertram and Lucille Jackson made their first appearance at The Church of the Evangelicals just this morning—"

"They did?"

"Yup, they came right down front and joined—"

"The nerve—"

"And it was very interesting to say the least—"

"Bet so."

"Well, in keeping with our plans," Gabe continued, "I'll schedule Jackson's first Trustee Training Class on next Monday evening—"

"Yup, and that'll get him out of my way." Gus nodded.

"But make sure no one gets hurt," Gabe said. "I'm still a preacher…and I can't abide anybody getting hurt—"

"The point of this operation is not to hurt anybody," Gus reminded the 4-Gs. "The point is to put fear into the hearts of these outcasts and misfits…and to run that Sheriff Jackson out o' town on a rail—"

"And by all that's right and holy, we'll elect Gus as sheriff." Greene's fat face blossomed to a beet red.

"And *Money Man*," Gus said, winking at Greg III. "You'll be out at your daddy's plant and putting yourself above all suspicion."

"Okay." Greg III nodded; even though his continued lack of full participation made him feel like a nerd and the low man on the totem pole—yet again.

"And as for you, *Radio Man*," Gus said, "you've got some important work to do. Greene, you've got to make a bunch of false police reports that'll spread the deputies out all over this county—"

"Got ya!" Greene grinned. "Then when I've done my job—"

"You'll play our favorite song on the radio," Gus said, "and I'll know it's my time to swing into action and send that church up in flames."

"This is station WSCM," Greene said, practicing his smooth delivery, "and this is one of your favorite cuts: 'A Mighty Fortress is our God'…jazzy style." His fat chin flapped as a surge of power and importance—the kind he'd always craved—thumped through his veins.

"But how will you do it, Gus?" Greg III couldn't resist fishing for details.

"Well," Gus said, taking a pompous stance, "I'll be dressed in all black, from head to toe, and wearing a hoodie. I'll sneak around to the back alley of the church and set the fire. There's a trash bin back there that'll do the trick. Afterwards, I'll have a cheap car, with stolen, out-of-state license plates, parked two or three streets over on The Presidents." Gus winked. "By the way, Greg III, I bought my getaway car at auction with your money."

"Sweet!" Greg III offered up a firm nod, finally feeling like a full-fledged member of the crew.

"And when the deed is done, I'll make a clean getaway," Gus continued, "easy-peezy…in…out…no one the wiser—"

"But how will we know you're alright?" Gabe countered. "How will we know you got away clean?"

"You'll know when you see my smiling face on TV, wearing my crisp chief deputy's uniform and answering questions about that *unfortunate* church fire to the press." Gus preened like he was practicing for the cameras. "You see, my boss, Sheriff Jackson, is not available to be on the scene of this tragic fire down here in The Presidents because he's way too busy uptown, taking silly classes at The Church of the Evangelicals from white folk who don't really want him around." Gus grinned and flashed the white-power sign. The other 4-Gs flashed back. The crew lounged around the picnic table; clanged their longnecks; and enjoyed a swelling belly laugh.

CHAPTER 13

Betsy Pritchard was getting seriously antsy. Molly had told her of her pregnancy several weeks ago, and she knew it wouldn't be long before she told her husband—and her daddy—and Betsy was frantic. Her husband had been asking her for days what was wrong. She couldn't eat; she couldn't sleep; she couldn't give her husband a straight answer.

"What's wrong, honey? You seem so distracted." Senior Pastor Pritchard posed to his wife at their breakfast table on the following Monday morning. "And it seems you've been that way for days—"

"Oh, it's nothing," Betsy said, staring down at her full plate of hash and eggs.

"It's not that thing with Lucille Jackson is it?"

"Huh?"

"It's not your fault, Betsy—"

"Yes, she is a troublesome woman," Betsy said, readily grasping at straws to explain her curious behavior.

"But it's not your fault that she was able to trick you into getting her husband an audience with me—"

"Yes, that's right. She is the tricky sort, isn't she?"

"And it's not your fault that the Jackson's joined our church on yesterday—"

"No?"

"No!" the pastor said. "If she hadn't worked the deal one way, she would've found a way to work it another."

"Guess you're right, honey—"

"And nothing you did gave them the nerve to come down front yesterday…on a blessed Sunday morning…and join our church—"

"Guess not—"

"That Lucille-woman was bound and determined to get it done. She's a social climber, and she feels like she has every right to set her black face inside a white church…trying to prove something, I guess—"

"But did you see Martha Jean Magpie?" Betsy ventured a slight chuckle. "I thought she would literally pass out—"

"And that's what she gets for wearing her corsets too tight." The preacher chuckled along with his wife, happy to see her improving spirits.

"I'm just glad that buffoon husband of hers…*Ex-Sheriff* Lester Magpie…wasn't in attendance. He would have definitely blown his gasket right there in the middle of the sanctuary—"

"Yes, he would've certainly blown up, just like the big windbag he is!" The preacher blew air into his cheeks until they were about to explode. "And that surely would've been a sight to see—"

"Tell me about it!" Betsy rewarded her husband's comic efforts with a girlish grin.

"Well, there's nothing much we can do about it now," the senior pastor said. "The deed is done. The Jacksons are members. But I'm having the deacons call all of our big tithers to reassure them that this might be short-lived. Because if Sheriff Jackson washes out of the lengthy and intensive Trustee Training Program, which has been developed by our fantastic son-in-law, Gabe, I think you'll see him haul his wife back down to Beulah Bible where they belong—"

"Trustee Training Program?" Betsy's mind had wandered.

"Oh, yes. I didn't tell you, did I? Gabe and I got things handled without having to involve the church's leadership," the preacher crowed. "You see, I had a follow-up meeting with Jackson in my church office last week. And I said, 'Sheriff Jackson, we would be delighted for you and your wife to become members of our church and, as you've clearly insisted, become a member of our leadership team…but under certain firm conditions.' And he said, 'Conditions?

What conditions? This is a church, ain't it? And we all have freewill, don't we?' And I said, 'Surely, it is a church, but we are a church with a very large operation. So, in order for you to hold down an office like Trustee, you must engage in a rigorous Trustee Training Program to get you ready for your new role.' And with a silly-looking expression on his face, he said, 'Huh?' He's been a deacon half his life, Betsy, but I guess the poor soul has never heard of church training—"

"Oh—"

"But then I told him the Trustee Training Program would run for six months with classes meeting on nights and weekends, and he had to achieve a score of 70% or above to pass the course," Senior Pastor Pritchard said, obviously proud of his skillful maneuvering. "Betsy, you should've seen Jackson, hemming and hawing and squirming around in my visitor's chair. I tell you that man's black face turned three shades of purple, but I patiently waited him out—"

"And—"

"And, finally, the man accepted," her husband said. "What else could he do? Not to accept would be to admit he's an incompetent coward...and no black man could ever do that. Consequently, we had Jackson between the crosshairs, and he caved-in and accepted our terms for becoming a member of our church and joining our leadership team."

"Oh—"

"Yes, it was priceless," the preacher said. "And I'm sure, before too long, Gabe's demanding curriculum will send that poor man running for the hills—"

"I'm sure you're right," Betsy responded dutifully, but her mind had long since fallen back to the problem at hand. Her fears were demanding immediate relief, and there was only one place she could get it before the secrets of her past blew up in all of their faces.

****

Betsy Pritchard never thought she'd be driving her late model Coupe de Ville Cadillac toward Lucille Jackson's side of town that afternoon. But there she was, bumping across the railroad tracks at breakneck speed, fumbling to locate an old address that she'd only frequented a few times in her distant past. It was after 3 p.m., and the schools had dismissed for the day. School children all along her route were exiting buses and waving fond farewells to their friends. Betsy was flustered and starting to get terribly confused; all of the old, run-down frame houses in The Presidents were starting to look the same.

Cora Lee Jackson lived where she'd always lived, on 3rd Avenue and Jefferson Street, just a few blocks over from Beulah Bible. She was sitting on her front porch, getting a breather after a long day in the Screamer High cafeteria, when Betsy Pritchard nearly took out a chunk of the sidewalk as she struggled to park.

"We've got to talk!" Betsy said, huffing her way up the sidewalk in Cora's direction. Her mousy brown hair was carelessly ruffled, and her normally kind, blue eyes were in a wild state of panic.

"Not here." Cora swung off her porch and met her halfway. She was a petite, coffee-colored woman with a short natural hairstyle and soulful brown eyes.

"Then where?" Betsy's wide eyes pled.

"Let's ride," Cora said and jumped in on the passenger side while Betsy resituated herself behind the wheel.

"The nerve of you to come stepping up to my house." Cora lit into her as soon as she was sure Betsy was in a fit state to drive. "Are you out o' your mind?"

"No!" Betsy jammed the brakes, nearly missing a red light. "Yes…I am just about out of my mind—"

"Why?" Cora questioned, keeping a sharp eye on the road in case she needed to take over.

"Because everything is falling apart!" Betsy's hands trembled on the steering wheel. "Everything is about to explode!"

"Just slow down and tell me what's wrong." Cora braced herself against Betsy's wild driving. "Head to the lake where we can stop and talk."

"Oh, okay." Betsy found her way to a quiet spot by Nolan Lake and jerked her car into park.

"Now, what is it? What's your problem?" Cora said as though she were speaking to one of the knot-head, rich kids at Screamer High.

"Molly's pregnant." Betsy broke. "My Molly is pregnant—"

"*Our* Molly is pregnant." Cora shifted in the seat so she could look directly at Betsy. "But what has you so upset—"

"Don't you get it!" Betsy's voice filled the car's void. "They're going to find out…they're all going to find out—"

"Oh, I see." Cora's mossy brown eyes filled with understanding. "You're scared—"

"Yes," Betsy admitted. "I'm scared to death—"

"You're scared that her baby…might be black—"

"I read somewhere…when an interracial couple has their first baby, it's more than a 50/50 chance that the baby will have white features—"

"But—"

"But…Molly and Gabe are talking about having a houseful of babies…and that…that would be a disaster—"

"For who?" Cora trapped Betsy in her smoldering eyes. "What's the disaster in having a houseful of babies—"

"But I haven't told her…I haven't told them…I haven't told my husband—"

"What?!?" Cora's hot breath fogged the windshield. "You swore to me that if my baby looked white, you'd adopt it—"

"I know," Betsy said, "and I kept my promise. I tried to do right by you—"

"But how did you adopt the baby if your husband doesn't even know?"

"My husband is a busy man." Betsy bristled. "He knew I had a lot of contacts in this area through my work with the Right-to-Life Movement. And I told him I'd make all the arrangements and handle all the details of the adoption if he'd just sign some papers—"

"And the po' man fell for that—"

"What else could he do? I'd had five miscarriages," Betsy said. "He knew I was fragile in this area. He was willing to do whatever it took to make me happy…to keep me sane—"

"And even after you handled everything, you never told your husband?" Cora sounded totally exasperated. "You never told the man that Molly's daddy is a white rapist, and her mother is a black woman?"

"No!" Betsy broke down in bitter tears. "No, I just never had the nerve to break it to him. I never could find the right time. And then Molly grew up…so bold, so brave, so beautiful—"

"So white—"

"I just didn't have the heart—"

"You're a coward, Betsy Prichard! And, now, you've got all of our lives trapped in your coward's web. What are you gonna do?"

"That's just it, Cora." Betsy trembled. "I don't know what to do. Please help me—"

"What're you expecting me to do?" Cora blasted. "Burst out like Super Woman and come in and save the day? I was raped…and my own brother, the Sheriff of Nolan County, doesn't even know. I had a child…and my own mama doesn't even know. I had a fiancé…and he dumped me because I couldn't let him know. And I dropped out o' college…because I could never recover from what I'd done. And I took a job…a menial job…at Screamer High so I could keep a close eye on my child…even if she never knew my name—"

"I'm sorry." Betsy sobbed. "I am so sorry that all this messed up your life—"

"And what of *our* Molly…our po' Molly…how's she gonna feel when she finds out she's a product of rape, and the only mother she's ever known is ashamed of her—"

"No!" Betsy wailed. "I'm not ashamed! I love my baby—"

"Then, what is it?" Cora narrowed her brown eyes, searching for the truth. "Is it her kinky, blonde hair? Is it her mismatched eyes—"

"No! No! I'm not ashamed...never ashamed…I love Molly just the way she is!" Betsy sobbed quietly. "I'm just stuck because I've allowed time to turn my secrets and half-truths into a lie…a big, fat lie!"

"That's the first honest thing you've said—"

"But that still doesn't change the fact that I've got to break the news to everyone," Betsy shrilled. "Oh! And what of Gabe…dear Gabe. How will he feel when he finds out that his wife—"

"Is half black—"

"Yes—"

"I knew the boy when he was at Screamer High…him, and his *4-G Crew*, or at least that's what they called themselves. They never got along well with the other kids. They're used to being outcasts. But I always had strong feelings for those four guys 'cause I know what it feels like not to fit in—"

"But when Gabe finds out that Molly is pregnant…and that their baby might look black…how will he feel then?"

"That's a toss-up—"

"What're you saying? Do you think I should just wait and see—"

"See what color the baby turns out to be—"

"Yes—"

"Now, Betsy, don't you think that's cutting it pretty close?" Cora eyeballed the white woman like she was a maniac. "What will you say if the baby's black—"

"But what if it's not—"

"But the next one might be—"

"And they'll find out…my husband…and the whole church—"

"Yup, the hard way—"

"Ohhhh…my poor head is spinning." Betsy cried. "This is too hard…just too, too hard—"

"Lies always are."

CHAPTER 14

Sirens were screaming when Assa Leckie, the lone black deputy sheriff, called into dispatch. "I've searched on 10th Avenue in The Presidents…from the top to the bottom." His radio squawked. "And there be no dead bodies lying around on the sidewalks down here, mon…none…no-wheres—"

"Forget that, Assa!" Lulabelle Stamps, who was on third shift at dispatch, shrilled uncharacteristically. "You get yourself down to 1st Avenue…near the railroad tracks! There's a three-alarm fire in progress in that strip shopping area. I think it's at that storefront church down there…Lordy mercy…and you're the closest one to the scene. The city needs our help, and all the other deputies are spread out on calls all over this county. Get right on down there; you hear me…uhh…10-4!"

Deputy Leckie arrived just in time to see yet another fire truck pulling on scene. "What's going on?" he yelled so that the fire chief could hear him over all of the commotion.

"I don't know," the fire chief yelled back, "but it's a hot one."

"Where did it start—"

"Looks like the blaze started in that storefront church…right over there." The fire chief pointed through the heavy smoke. "Do you happen to know the preacher?"

"Yeah," Leckie said, "I know of Bishop Pride. Has anybody called him?"

"I don't know," Fire Chief Vanderpool said as he ran over to support his men who were battling the fierce blaze. "That's your job…mine is to get this monster under control before it burns down this whole strip—"

"Dispatch!" Deputy Leckie's radio squawked. "Where be Sheriff Jackson?"

"He's in route!" Lulabelle blared.

"Okay, I will remain here until he arrives," Leckie said. "But you call the Bishop Pride and tell him to get down here right away…his church be up in flames…10-4!" Leckie watched as the WRBL news trucks pulled up, and he directed them to a safe area to park away from the intense heat of the fire. As soon as the news reporters were in place, Chief Deputy Gus McVey arrived on the scene. "Uh-huh," Leckie mumbled to himself. "Might've known this mon, here, would be coming just in time to cheese it up with the press. I do not trust that white mon. He be the worst of the breed."

"I'm standing here, as you can see, with flames raging in the background at this four-alarm fire at the strip shopping center on 1st Avenue and Ann Street in Screamer, South Carolina. Since Sheriff Jackson has not yet arrived on the scene, I'm speaking with Chief Deputy Gus McVey," the perky news reporter announced to her viewers. "Chief Deputy McVey, what is the situation as you know it?"

"Good evening." Gus pursed his thick lips for the television cameras. "It's bad…very bad. Nothing like this has ever happened in Screamer before. It's unprecedented." He ran his fingers through his blonde hair in dismay. "But, right now, the fire chief and his crew are working tirelessly to bring this fire under control. It appears to have started in the church over there…think they call it…Holy Ghost Headquarters…and the fire officials are trying to keep the fire contained in that area so that it doesn't spread to endanger the other businesses in this strip shopping center. That's all we know for now, but we'll be here until the fire department completes its mission."

"Where is Sheriff Jackson?" the news reporter queried. "Why isn't he on the scene?"

"Oh…I can't really say for sure," Gus said, attempting to sound loyal to his conspicuously absent boss. "But I think he's probably just stuck in his class…uptown…at The Church of the Evangelicals. But I'm sure…very sure…he's on his way—"

"Do you think the fire was arson…caused by person or persons unknown?" the news reporter said, prodding for details.

"There's no way of knowing that for sure right now. The fire's burning way too hot." Gus looked straight into the camera for the benefit of his 4-G Crew. "But you can believe we'll investigate this fire right away. And if it's arson," he added, "the party or parties involved will be swiftly apprehended and brought to justice." Gus curled his lips and discreetly displayed the secret white-power sign before his face went out of frame.

The remainder of the 4-G Crew, who were glued to the television broadcast, returned their buddy's white-power sign with a feeling of enormous pride. *Hooray! We did it! Mission accomplished!*

****

It was an extremely long and grueling night. Sheriff Jackson didn't return home until nearly 3 a.m., but Lucille was waiting up for him. "Bertram, are you alright?" Lucille started in on him in an anxious whisper. "Is everybody alright?"

"Yeah, baby," the sheriff said, dragging. "Can we talk about it over breakfast? I need some sleep—"

"But…where were you?" Lucille persisted.

"Huh?"

"Why weren't you available for the 10 o'clock news cameras?" Lucille quizzed. "Why did they interview Gus McVey about the fire and not you?"

"When I was notified, the fire was in progress," the weary sheriff said. "I was in my Trustee Training Class all the way uptown at The Church of the Evangelicals…and it took me a minute to break away and get there—"

"But it looked bad…you not being on the scene to conduct the interview—"

"Lucille, can we take this up again when I've had some rest," the sheriff said as he flopped into his arm chair to remove his sooty boots."

"Well, was it arson?"

"There's no way for us to know until the fire chief completes his investigation but—"

"But—"

"But Deputy Leckie was the first on scene, and he definitely thinks it was arson since there was nobody in the church at the time—"

"Well, thank God for that," Lucille said. "But what're you going to do about it, Bertram?"

"We're going to finish our investigation…before we go off half-cocked—"

"But you're the Sheriff of Nolan County, now…a black man. And somebody's gotta remind these crazy rednecks that they're not the only ones with torches and guns!"

"And even if it was arson, Lucille, we don't know it was about race—"

"Of course, it's about race," Lucille said. "It's always about race!"

"Even if this fire was racially motivated, we can't do anything about—"

"Oh, yes, you can! You can most certainly do something about it. You're the sheriff—"

"What I was getting ready to say, Lucille," her husband said, jaws cracking, "we can't do anything about how white folk hate us. We've got to get over ever expecting white folks to love us and start loving ourselves and each other—"

"Whatcha mean?"

"When we begin to have the kind of unity and solidarity we need from within, we'll have the show of strength necessary to deal with the enemy without—"

"Make sense, Bertram—"

"What I'm saying is…when we as black folk show ourselves as a unified, solid front, people will have to think twice before getting in our faces or destroying our property. But, right now, it doesn't seem like black folk even love each other anymore." The sheriff dropped out of his heavy clothes. "You'd be surprised at the black-on-black crimes I have to deal with in this little town every day." The sheriff's tired head drooped. "And not even the black churches seem to be getting along—"

"But—"

"And now you've moved us uptown to some white church just so you can get the chance to spit in their eye—"

"It's our right—"

"Yes, honey, it's most definitely our right." Sheriff Jackson drug himself toward the hot shower his body craved. "But I'm trying to show you that hatred and racism run both ways…*you hit my dog; I kick yo' cat*. But we won't make any kind of progress that way, and we won't have any kind of life that way. This two-headed monster has devilish roots…and it's destructive to everyone. When will it ever end?"

CHAPTER 15

Since he and Lucille had moved their membership, Sheriff Jackson had no way of knowing that Pastor Renfrow of Beulah Bible had called a meeting of all the black pastors in Screamer, bright and early on the Tuesday morning following the horrendous fire. There was no more time for skirting the issues or trying to handle their mutual problems singlehandedly. Pastor Renfrow believed that the silo effect that is so prevalent in the modern-day Christian church—those subtle, unaddressed hatreds allowed to fester along racial and denominational lines—had to be addressed head-on and dealt with before they could do any more harm in Screamer.

As he witnessed the changing times, Pastor Renfrow had been so deeply moved by the growing factions among the churches in Screamer that he'd burned the midnight oil to research the topic. The current state of affairs—churches divided on the basis of status, race, culture, gender, or any other such thing—was one that the Apostle Paul, the New Testament's greatest church founder, would certainly have abhorred. He would've been the first to take a stand against so-called Christian churches for behaving so un-Christlike.

Pastor Renfrow's study had landed him squarely in the Book of Galatians where the Apostle Paul had proved his firm stance on such matters when he "withstood Peter to the face". He called-out his fellow laborer in the gospel, the Apostle Peter, for attempting to place an unholy division between Jewish and Gentile believers. Paul admonished him that while the ways in which we're called to faith may vary with each individual, we are all saved into the Kingdom of God in the exact same way—by faith alone in Christ alone—and not by any human effort. The blood that Jesus shed on the cross paid for the sins of the whole world—past, present, and future—and His resurrection from the grave is proof that God accepted His sacrifice. Things like position, power, money, ethnic origin, good works, or any other worldly distinctions that attempt to set us apart from each other have absolutely no value and no place in the body of Christ. Paul made it clear that all true believers are made to be one in Christ because our Lord and Saviour is not a respecter of persons.

Pastor Renfrow sincerely believed these simple Bible truths, and they had taken him to his knees in the wee-morning hours of the regrettable fire. In prayer, he realized that maybe the fire was not so much a disaster as it was a wake-up call—a time to eradicate the two-headed monster that had been allowed to thrive for too long in Screamer. *If God's people want to see God's power, then we have to do God's will God's way. It's the church's job to repent first and put Jesus Christ back in His rightful place...back on the throne of each one of our hearts. Then, He'll give us the power to reach the world. And now, more than ever, the welfare and safety of black lives in The Presidents depends on it.*

"Bishop Pride, we are all so sorry for your loss," Pastor Renfrow said as he greeted the other two pastors into his office with a sincere and solemn face.

"Thank you, Pastor," Bishop Pride responded soberly as he took a seat around Pastor Renfrow's round conference table. There was no head seat at his table, and the three pastors came casually dressed for the occasion. "The fire caused a complete and utter destruction of our physical plant and the loss of all of our church property," Bishop Pride said. "And my congregation is suffering the intense pain and agony of our loss, to say the least, but we are indeed grateful to God that there was no loss of life."

"Yes, Lord," Pastor Shaundra Strong said, taking her seat alongside him at the large conference table. "And, Bishop, the entire community is so very sorry for your loss and that of your congregation's at Holy Ghost Headquarters."

"Thank you kindly for your concern, Sister Strong." The bishop nodded, disregarding her office.

"But if this fire is found to be arson," Pastor Renfrow stated plainly, "it is a very distinct possibility that the black folk in The Presidents are going to blow up in a fit of rage—"

"Especially if the fire was set by some…some white racists!" Bishop Pride boomed.

"I hear tell that the chief deputy…that mean white man…has been putting lots of strong pressure on the young folk down here lately…especially the young men and boys—"

"And this fire is just the kind of thing to set off all the growing tensions in The Presidents like a timebomb—"

"I know, and we can't take that risk," Pastor Strong said. "Too many innocent young people are liable to get hurt."

"But if we're going to talk about this tragedy in earnest today," Pastor Renfrow said, shifting uncomfortably, "I think it requires us to act like the brothers and sisters in Christ that we truly are…put all of our cards on the table…be transparent with one another. Don't you agree?"

"Yes." The other two pastors nodded their assent, clearly aware of their brother's holy intentions.

"If we, the leaders and pastors of our flocks, can't get together as children of God," Pastor Renfrow said, "how can we ever expect to lead God's people or draw unbelievers to accept the claims of Christ and the love that He offers?" Pastor Renfrow was intentional in his delivery, but he was doing his level best not to preach. "If we are jealous, and spiteful, and envious, and generally hateful toward one another on earth, why would anyone, looking from the outside in, want to enter into the Kingdom of Heaven?"

"You are right, Brother Pastor; you're so right," the other two pastors shamefacedly agreed.

"Then…I guess it behooves me to go first," the bishop said, shifting his eyes down toward the table. "A-hem…I guess it's no secret that my denomination does not believe in women pastors."

"No secret." Pastor Shaundra Strong nodded in a quiet whisper.

"Indeed." Pastor Renfrow nodded. However, based on his exhaustive study of the Bible, he wasn't exactly in favor of women pastors, either; especially when it came to single, fine-looking women like Shaundra Strong having to counsel knot-head single men and hen-pecked married couples. Women preachers, teachers, and evangelists, sure; but pastors, well, he was still somewhat on the fence. But one thing was sure, Pastor Renfrow was solidly against anything that divided believers, and he was not about to take up his minor unreadiness with the other staunch nitpickers and heartless naysayers whose objections were often fueled by jealousy and other petty motives.

"And I would like to go on record as saying that I do subscribe to all of our denomination's beliefs," the bishop said flatly. "But I'm beginning to see…in perilous times such as these…we cannot allow our denominational biases to separate us as the children of God." The bishop looked squarely into the preacher's lovely brown eyes. "So…Sister…Pastor Strong…let me be the first to apologize. If my harsh stand on this point has been a source of strain and offence to you over the years, I do, now, sincerely apologize."

"I'm glad to hear you say that Bishop." Pastor Strong's rosebud lips turned upward into a sweet smile. "And I do understand your denomination's stand on the issue. But I've been talking it over with my leadership, and we, too, believe it's high-time for solidarity. We've been talking on the phone throughout this dark night in Screamer…with tears in our hearts…and I've been authorized to make you an offer—"

"Oh?" The bishop gaped.

"First and foremost, we are firm believers in Jesus Christ, and whether we agree on every point or not, we have the same Father;

we worship the same Lord; and that makes us brothers and sisters in Christ," Pastor Strong said. "And, as such, Mount Olive would like to extend an olive branch, of sorts, and invite you, Bishop, and your entire congregation, to share our sanctuary during this, your time of need—"

"Well—"

"I know you'll have to check with your leadership before making such a decision, but we just want you to know that you are welcomed to fellowship with us at Mount Olive until you've rebuilt or found another suitable location—"

"Your generosity of spirit overwhelms me, Pastor Strong." The bishop wobbled uncharacteristically. "I find myself speechless at this time, and I'm sure my membership will be deeply grateful and moved by your offer as well…whether my Elder Board agrees to accept it or not.

"You're welcome, Bishop Pride," Pastor Strong said with a kind smile, knowing what strength of character and faith it had taken to bring him to a point of reversal. "We, at Mount Olive, just want you to know our offer is sincere; our doors and our hearts are open; and we await your response."

"Well, this meeting has gone much better than I could've ever expected." Pastor Renfrow sat at the table in awe, overwhelmed by the mighty move of the Spirit that he'd just witnessed. *For where two or three are gathered together in my name, there am I in the midst of them.* "It just goes to show us that it takes the Lord to plow-up the stony ground of our hearts…in whatever manner He sees fit…in order to sow new seeds of understanding—"

"Yes, making us uncomfortable is sometimes the first step to making us grow—"

"And if it took the pain of a violent church fire to help us come together and find common ground…maybe…somehow…it'll all be worth it in the end." Pastor Renfrow cast a sympathetic eye toward Bishop Pride. "Because I'm encouraged that if the three of us can make peace, we can build solidarity in the black community to carry us through this trying time. And, hopefully, we can find ways to come out of this tragedy much better than before."

"Amen."

In closing, the three pastors stood together in unity. Pastor Renfrow locked hands with his fellow ministers of the gospel and prayed, "I declare, in the precious name of Jesus, that the enemy will not win. And, Lord, we know you will bless our efforts and show us favor as we find it in our hearts to fulfil Your royal mission…to live justly, to be merciful, and to love one another."

CHAPTER 16

"What took you so long?" Greene railed as the 4-G Crew settled down in their favorite spot by Nolan Lake. "It's been over a week since the fire—"

"I waited to get us back together…wanted to be sure the coast was clear," Gus said. "Besides, I had some other important stuff to do—"

"Oh, yeah!" Greene spit out a wry chuckle. "What could be more important than burning that black church down to the ground?"

"I'll get to that," Gus said, "but, first, what were your thoughts on our operation—"

"Uhh…the fire?" Greg III asked in his characteristically dufus style.

"Yeah, the fire!" Gus blared. "Of course, the fire—"

"Calm down," Gabe said, "we don't want anyone overhearing us, do we?"

"You're right." Gus raised his hands and lowered his tone. "Well, what did you think?"

"It was fabulous!" Greene praised his pal. "It was phenomenal!"

"Burned that sucker right down to the ground—"

"And without much damage to the adjacent stores—"

"And that was good." Gabe nodded. "That…and the fact that no one got hurt—"

"It was freaking stupendous!" Gus roared. "Even if I do say so myself!"

"So…what did the WNL have to say?" Greg III persisted with his bothersome questions. "Did we score any points with them?"

"Did we?" Gus swooned. "They were absolutely over the moon with our whole operation. We did it just right!"

"We busted some heads—"

"And we got away scot-free!"

"But tell us…what exactly did our unit prez have to say?" Gabe took a perch on top of the picnic table.

"Clive said he heard from the Grand Master on the very night of the fire," Gus said, detailing their conversation. "And according to him, the Grand Master said two more winners like that, and we'll be inducted into his Inner Court—"

"The Inner Court of the WNL! WOW!" Greene cheered, but he was eyeing the empty grill. His mouth was watering for some steaks and beer to celebrate.

"That's what we're all after, remember?" Gus said. "That…and getting me elected sheriff, right?"

"Right!"

"So, Gus, what was the other important thing you've been up to?" Gabe said, bringing them back on point.

"It wasn't just important It was *terribly* important!" Gus strutted around the picnic table like a proud peacock. "Are you guys ready for this?"

"What?"

"I found my daddy!" Gus bellowed, jumped up and down, and danced a lively jig.

"You did what?!?"

"Yes! Yes! That *white* guy in my mom's picture …well, he's my daddy—"

"But how do you know?"

"It took some real detective work for sure." Gus set his thick lips into a familiar smirk. "But then, that's what I do—"

"What did you do—"

"First of all, I found my daddy's picture in the statewide law enforcement database—"

"He's a criminal—"

"He was a criminal—"

"He's out?"

"Naw, he's dead." Gus spat on the ground and scrubbed it out under his work boot. "Second, I was able to check my DNA against the DNA in his prison records—"

"I didn't know you could do that—"

"You're not supposed to do that." Gus flashed Greg III a disapproving side-eye for the interruption. "But I've got a buddy down at the lab who owed me a serious favor…for not spilling the beans to his wife—"

"About what?"

"Never mind, Greg III!" Greene said. "Let the man tell his story, geez!"

"And the lab tech ran your DNA against the white guy's in the picture?" Gabe filled in the blanks.

"Yes!" Gus paced, too giddy to keep still. "And it was a match…it was a perfect match!"

"So…why's he dead…your daddy, I mean?" Greg III dared ask.

"After serving 12 years on death row, he was sent to the electric chair a few years back—"

"The electric chair?"

"For what?"

"What in the world did he do?" Greg III wiped his foggy glasses and reseated them.

"He was convicted of rape and murder—"

"Rape?"

"And murder?"

"His name was George McManus, and the cops investigating the case nicknamed him…The Shutter-Bug Rapist—"

"The Shutter-Bug Rapist—"

"Whoa!"

"That's 'cause he kept pictures of himself at each one of his crime scenes—"

"Every time he raped a woman?"

"Yeah." Gus scrubbed his blonde head with a hard fist. "And that's what got him caught…those stupid trophy pictures. The police found them in his possession when he was picked up, and at least five of the girls were able to I.D. him and the photo that he'd taken of himself at the scene of the crime—"

"But who did he murder?" Greg III succumbed to his appetite for details.

"Must've been his very first victim. He must've bound and gagged her too tight," Gus said. "But after that, he only blitzed his unsuspecting victims with a surprise attack. That's why so many of the girls were able to identify him. He didn't even try to hide his face. They think there must've been twelve in total—"

"But how could they know that?"

"The silly fool kept a scrapbook." Gus tossed a pebble out toward the lake. "There were eleven crime scene pictures of himself in his scrapbook, but it looked like one of them was missing…so they think there must've been twelve—"

"Do you think the picture you found of him standing in front of that church…the one with the stained-glass window…is the missing crime scene photo?" Gabe asked.

"Might be—"

"Sorry about this, Gus," Greene said, searching for the right words to console his friend.

"It's not every day a cop finds out his own daddy—" Greg III bit his tongue in mid-sentence.

"Is a rapist and murderer," Gabe said, completing the thought.

"It's got nothing to do with me." Gus shrugged. "That was his doing, not mine. The only thing I know for absolute sure is that this man…this *white* man…was my daddy. And that's good enough for me!" Gus issued each of his 4-G pals a copy of the picture. "This is George McManus," he said proudly. "This is my daddy."

"Well, now, you can put all that worry and doubt to rest, right?" Gabe said, proud to see his friend taking his mixed-blessing so well.

"That's right!" Gus slapped his knee. "And, now, it's on to new business—"

"What?"

"The next church will burn to the ground next Friday night—"

"Friday night?"

"Yeah, we've gotta switch it up on 'em—"

"Which one?"

"The one they call Mount Olive goes up next," Gus said, "and we'll save the one they love the best for last…Beulah Bible—"

"How will we do it?

"Same as last time," Gus said, spitting out orders. "Preacher Man, get that Bertram Jackson over to a Trustee Training Class next Friday evening."

"That'll be no problem," Gabe said. "I've got him convinced that his time in Trustee Training is a community service of sorts; especially in times like these when tempers in The Presidents are on such a short fuse. I've got him thinking that his membership at our church will go a long way toward furthering better race relations between blacks and whites in Screamer—"

"Ha-Ha-Ha! Fool!" Gus doubled over in spiteful laughter. "And Radio Man, we need you to call in some more of those fake incident reports to get those deputies hopping all over Nolan County—"

"And when I'm done," Greene said, chin fat flapping, "I'll get to play our very favorite song…'A Mighty Fortress is our God'…jazzy style!"

"Right!" Gus grinned. "And Greg III, you stay well out o' the way; do you hear me? You keep working hard at the mill 'cause we'll be needing some more of your daddy's hard-earned cash real soon!"

"Yes, Gus, I hear you." Greg III nodded, grateful to have such a tight-knit group of friends; even though, from time to time, he felt like the black sheep of the bunch. "I know; I know. I'm just the Money Man—"

"And the Money Man is important, too," Gabe said, offering his friend a quick nod and a word of comfort.

"Everybody clear on your roles?" Gus McVey grinned. "We'll get this one done in honor of my newly-found daddy…George McManus…a *white* man!"

"Yessss!"

"Then let's do it!" Gus chanted while making a tight victory lap. "We'll burn down another one—"

"Just like the other one!" They all whooped and flashed the white-power sign like four wicked little boys.

****

Since Mount Olive and Holy Ghost Headquarters had combined after the fire, Pastor Shaundra Strong's office had become the busy nerve center for the operation. Careful not to ruffle any feathers in the mixed multitude, the seasoned community leader cleared her office when she received a telephone call from Pastor Renfrow.

"How are things going over there?" Pastor Renfrow attempted to sound chatty when he reached out to Mount Olive's beautiful, yet spiritual, Pastor Shaundra Strong.

"Is this just a social call, Pastor?"

"Well, I guess not," Pastor Renfrow said. "It's been a few weeks since Mount Olive and Holy Ghost Headquarters combined after the fire. And I must admit, I've been a little fleshly curious and Holy Ghost concerned about how things are going between you and Bishop Pride."

"I understand." Pastor Shaundra giggled and eased her respected colleague off the hook. "I've been expecting your call—"

"Well—"

"Well, to tell the truth, the blended family of Mount Olive and Holy Ghost Headquarters is having some serious growing pains—"

"I can only imagine—"

"Our sisters wear pants—"

"And there's don't—"

"They shout—"

"And y'all don't—"

"We have Sunday School—"

"And they don't." Pastor Renfrow's voice smiled.

"Oh, and we have Bible Study on Wednesday nights—"

"And they have it on Thursdays—"

"Yes, silly little stuff like that has been causing some major eye-straining and head-turning betwixt our two congregations," Pastor Shaundra said. "But, other than that, the saints have been pretty respectful one to the other—"

"So…how are you and the Bishop working it out?"

"Well, we've agreed that I'll preach on first and third Sundays, and Bishop Pride will preach on second and fourth—"

"Ladies first, I guess?"

"Something like that." Pastor Shaundra chuckled. "But on fifth Sundays, we'll have a combined Youth Rally. So, that way, folk can decide what Sundays they desire to attend and how much of this *mixing* they can tolerate."

"And the giving?"

"We're using two separate envelopes for the tithes and offerings," Pastor Strong said, "so, we don't expect any issues—"

"Well, I think that's commendable."

"And I'm starting to think that this forced union is making both congregations stronger in the ways of the Lord—"

"In the ways of love?" Pastor Renfrow restated.

"In the ways of love," Pastor Shaundra agreed. "After all, we worship and serve the same Jesus."

"You know," Pastor Renfrow said, shifting the subject, "the fire chief has ruled that the church fire was definitely arson—"

"What kind of low-down creature could burn down God's house of worship?"

"The lowest kind—"

"And everybody down here feels like it was racially motivated," Pastor Strong said. "All the young people in The Presidents were planning a big protest rally…planning to march downtown and let Sheriff Jackson know just how strongly they feel about it. But I'm glad it fizzled out somehow because the way tempers are flaring, that could've turned into a riot!"

"Our Sheriff Jackson is no fool. I've known him his whole life." Pastor Renfrow attempted to relieve her concerns. "He may be going uptown to The Church of the Evangelicals right now, but he knows that him and his whole Sheriff's Department are on the hot seat right down here in The Presidents."

"That's good to know."

"And I think the young folk have cooled down a bit just by seeing your two churches…on opposite ends of the denominational divide…come together to support each other at a time like this. And besides that, the Bishop has been very outspoken on his stance for tolerance and peace.

"I think you're right, Pastor Renfrow. If us church folk ain't clowning and acting the fool, it makes our young people feel they don't need to do it either. That is…unless it happens again—"

"Heaven forbid!"

"God forbid!"

"We've got to pray and do everything in our power to prevent that from happening." Pastor Renfrow sighed. "It's a shame, too. White folk just *do not* play well with others. They never have—"

"Yeah, you're right. Maybe, it's their burden to have some sort of superiority complex. But I know one thing for sure, these white racists better quit fooling around down here before they wake up Pookie and 'em…even the folk in The Presidents don't mess with Pookie. If that wild bunch ever gets up a real head of steam, all the prayers in the world won't hold back their brand of crazy—"

"They see themselves as the guardians of The Presidents," Pastor Renfrow said. "And if these white cowards persist in burning our churches, they're subject to get the repeat of the Civil War they've been itching for—"

"Yes, sir!" Pastor Shaundra's voice swelled. "Pookie and his crew are subject to go uptown and do some real damage. We want equal justice and equal rights; they want revenge, and they don't mind dying for it. They'll be on top o' them white fools before they can even get their big guns cocked…and there will be blood in these streets!"

"Well, we surely don't want that," Pastor Renfrow said. "I've been talking to Deputy Assa Leckie, who's a member of my flock, about keeping a much tighter eye on things down here. Too many innocent, young lives could be lost if The Presidents ever erupt in violence—"

"And if that were to happen, it would play right into the hands of this hateful, murderous, lying spirit that satan has unleashed in the world—"

"And we don't want our children dead in the streets—"

"We want them to live—"

"To get to know Jesus—"

"To get saved—"

"To be a blessing—"

"To live long and prosper—

"To see a brighter day—"

"Yes, Lord!" the two pastors shouted in strong agreement.

CHAPTER 17

"No tea this time, Mommy?" Molly's voice sparkled as brightly as her multi-colored eyes when she met with her mother under the sprawling covered veranda. It was another splendid South Carolina day in May.

"No, baby…no tea this time." Betsy Pritchard's dainty white hands shook noticeably. "Thought we might need a cocktail for our lunch today." There were finger sandwiches and mint juleps, replete with a sprig of mint, set at each of the lovely place settings. A plain, brown manilla envelope was on Betsy's side of the table. She'd also given her maid, Maude, the afternoon off.

"Isn't it a little early in the day for cocktails, Mommy?" Molly giggled, attempting to lighten the mood. "Besides, I'm pregnant; you know—"

"I'll let you decide." Betsy's head drooped.

"What's wrong, Mommy?" Molly sat up erectly in her brightly-cushioned, wrought-iron chair. "Are you alright?"

"I won't know," Betsy said, "not until I find the nerve to tell you what I need to say—"

"What is it, Mommy? You're scaring me." Molly's mismatched eyes flickered like the great northern lights. "You know you can tell me anything—"

"Oh, my dear child, where do I begin?" Betsy's face tensed into a tight white ball. "You see, this story all started after I'd had five miscarriages trying to give birth to my own babies—"

"I know all about that—"

"No, Molly, you don't!" Betsy cut her daughter short and took a long draw from her mint julep. She placed her hands over the plain, brown manilla envelope and set her gentle blue eyes onto the table.

Then she told Molly the truth—the whole truth—from woeful beginning to tearful end.

"So…you're telling me…my mother…my birth mother…is a black woman?" Molly's crystal blue eye was having one reaction, and her mossy brown one quite another. The conflict was making her feel sick to her stomach, and both of her eyes were flooded with hot, unshed tears.

"Yes, I'm afraid so." Betsy's petite body quivered.

"And…let me get this straight." A single tear finally rolled out of Molly's blue eye. "This black woman…who's my birth mother…she was raped?"

"Yes." Betsy trembled, unable to meet Molly's gaze.

"So…my daddy…my real…blood daddy…is a white rapist!?!" Molly's voice rose from a low rumble to an ear-splitting shrill with each passing syllable.

"I am so sorry, Molly," Betsy whispered, shaking uncontrollably. "Yes…it's true…it's all true—"

"True?" Molly blared. "What could you possibly know about the truth?!?"

"But-but, Molly, I was only trying to protect you—"

"No! No! Betsy Pritchard…you weren't trying to protect me! You were trying to protect yourself!" Molly pressed back her tears with her plaid cloth napkin. "You were trying to protect the lie you'd perfected over the 23 years of my life!"

"But—"

"I don't mind who I am." Molly stopped her cold with a flash of her napkin. "I can't do anything about that. That's the Lord's choice. That's who He made me." Her dual eyes rolled in violent waves, like thunder and lightning on a stormy night. "But I hate the fact that you didn't trust me enough…didn't love me enough…to ever tell me the truth—"

"But, Molly, I do love you—"

"You raised me to speak my mind and to tell the truth…even if it hurt!" Molly blasted. "While all the time you couldn't find it in your own heart to speak the truth to me…not even once—"

"But…but I'm telling you, now—" Betsy's breath crashed across her chest in violent sobs.

"Only because you have to." Molly's brown eye was smoldering like a sliver of burnished steel while the blue one was doing its best to cool it down. "Only because I'm pregnant, and you're afraid of how my baby…my precious, darling baby…might look—"

"It's not that! It's not that!"

"Then what is it?"

"I just can't hold my peace any longer—"

"So…who is this man…my daddy, I mean? What's his name?"

"I don't know—"

"Not even to this day—"

"No!" Betsy wailed. "We do not know—"

"Then what's in the envelope?"

"Well…it's…it's a picture—"

"Of what?"

"Not what?" Betsy's voice quaked. "Who?" she said as she slid the plain, brown manilla envelope over to Molly's side of the table.

Molly slurped a sip of her mint julep, against her better judgment, and tore open the envelope. "Isn't this…*The Lunchroom Lady*?" Molly's eyes re-scrambled. "Why are you showing me a picture of The Lunchroom Lady?"

"That's Cora Lee Jackson." Betsy swallowed hard over the herd of elephants stampeding in her throat. "That's your mother…your birth mother." It was the picture of a young Cora, smiling in front of Beulah Bible.

"Are you telling me—" Molly's strained words failed her, and she slumped over the table; her belly was seizing with pain.

"Are you okay?" Betsy said, wishing she could somehow bear her daughter's anguish.

"Are you saying…The Lunchroom Lady…who I have known nearly half my life…is my birth mother?!?"

"Yes." It was the single word Betsy Pritchard dared utter.

"How could you?" Molly shuttered; her mismatched eyes were drowning in tears. This revelation was almost more than she could bear. Her intense emotions were ripping her insides to pieces. "How could the two of you keep such a painful, hurtful secret from me…all of the days of my life. How could you?"

"I'm so sorry, Molly." Betsy trembled, attempting to push back her own tears. "I…we…never meant to hurt you…never, never—"

"And Daddy…your husband…he went along with this sham?"

"He doesn't know—"

"He doesn't know!" Molly's two-toned eyes twirled violently. "You've been married to the man nearly 50 years, and you never bothered to tell him the tragedy of my birth?!?"

"He…I—" Betsy stammered badly. "I've never thought of your birth as a tragedy, Molly Anne, and I thought…one day…we'd tell him together—"

"Molly Anne?" She slumped into her chair like a battered rag doll. Everything she'd ever known—had ever taken as gospel—was crumbling right before her tortured eyes. "Is that even my real name?"

"Yes, Molly," Betsy said, struggling to regain her own equilibrium. "I gave you that name…and Cora agreed before she signed the papers for your adoption—"

"Oh! Oh!" Molly cried; her head felt like a walnut being cracked wide open.

"Have you told Gabe about the baby, yet?" Betsy dared ask.

"No, I have not!" Molly passed one shaky hand across Cora's face—lovingly—as though she were touching her own mother for the very first time. "And, now, I won't tell him," her voice hollowed, "I can't tell him…not until after—"

"After what, my dear?"
"After I talk to...*The Lunchroom Lady*—"

CHAPTER 18

Deputy Assa Leckie's left hand was tingling and his right eye was twitching. And since he was a boy in Gullah-land, that signaled trouble. Besides, Sheriff Jackson had lowered the boom on the whole squad at Friday morning roll call, and his commanding voice was still ping-ponging around in Leckie's skull.

"You deputies have gotta put your hearts and shields on the line!" Sheriff Jackson's shouts had rattled the blinds and broken the sound barrier in the tight confines of the squad room. "You've gotta double down and apprehend the person or persons who perpetrated this heinous crime…whoever set that horrible fire at Holy Ghost Headquarters. It's just a blessing nobody got seriously hurt, and it's a slap in the face to our whole department. Now it's our sworn duty to find the cowards, make 'em pay, and make sure nothing like this ever happens again in Nolan County!"

"Yes, sir, boss!" Chief Deputy Gus McVey rallied the troops and led the cheers of affirmation.

Consequently, Deputy Leckie was doubling down and putting his heart and shield on the line when dispatch blasted over his radio. "Leckie, what's your 20; come back."

"I'm out here near the *Welcome to Screamer* sign, running a radar check," the deputy said.

"Well, drop that," the dispatcher barked, "we've got a report of shots fired over near Nolan State Park—"

"Find you another," Deputy Leckie retorted. "Speed kills, and I'm out here saving me some lives…10-4."

But the one place Deputy Leckie was not was out near the *Welcome to Screamer* sign. He'd fudged his location. For, in fact, he was running a loose stakeout that Friday evening between Beulah

Bible and Mount Olive because he'd made a solemn promise to Pastor Renfrow to keep a close eye on things. "I will do my level best, my pastor, to keep another church from going up in flames," he'd said. "I love The Presidents and all of its people. I want no riot to break out down here…no, mon, not on my watch."

Deputy Leckie was making his second or third drive-by around 8 p.m. at Mount Olive when he spotted something that looked suspicious. It was a sudden burst of light that flared and subsided near the rear of the church in the Fellowship Hall area. The deputy killed his patrol car's engine and lights and waited a few minutes in the dark. There was only one pole light on that stretch of Jefferson Street, and it was on the opposite end of the block. Under the cover of darkness, the deputy could see movement around the church. He eased out of his car, without closing the door, and inched his way toward the image dressed in black.

"Stop! Police!" Deputy Leckie shouted, but the startled person draped in a black hoodie dropped an object and took off on foot.

Leckie followed in hot foot pursuit for two blocks, over to Washington Street. When Leckie finally caught up, the suspect was fleeing the scene in an old Buick with an Illinois state license plate. Leckie was perturbed that he was only able to get a partial plate number, but he committed it to memory on the spot. Winded, he didn't stop to rest. He made a return run to Mount Olive to see what the suspect had left behind. But when he arrived, the rear of the Fellowship Hall was already in flames.

"Dispatch!" Deputy Leckie shrilled over his radio. "Send fire trucks to Mount Olive down here in The Presidents, and do it with a quickness, mon! The church, it be in flames! The church is on fire! Get here now…10-4!"

The fire was at three alarms by the time Sheriff Jackson arrived. "What happened, Leckie? the sheriff said. "What're you up to?"

"I be here on the job…where you be?" A weary Deputy Leckie gave a tight tug on his service cap—the one which he was never without around his fellow officers.

"I was uptown…at my class at The Church of the Evangelicals when I received the call," the sheriff said, resenting his deputy's insolence. "But I'm here now; so, what went down?"

"I saw someone lurking around the back of the church—"

"No…let's start with why were you down here in the first place?" The sheriff retorted. "My report shows you out near the *Welcome to Screamer* sign—"

"I was doing what you told us to do, Sheriff," Leckie said. "I was putting my heart and shield on the line to keep these black churches safe in The Presidents. That's what you instructed us to do, is it not?"

"We'll talk about your insubordination later," the sheriff said, shoulders tightly knotted, "but what did you see?"

"I saw me someone, dressed in a black hoodie, skulking around the back side of the church over there." The deputy pointed to the spot where the fire trucks had parked. "When the person see me, they run. They run for their life. I give chase two blocks over to Washington, and then they jump into an old Buick and tore out of there—"

"Did you get the license plate—"

"Partial." Leckie nodded. "It was an Illinois plate, and it started with RVS-1…sorry…could not read the rest as the car sped away—"

"That helps." Sheriff Jackson relaxed his shoulders.

"I picked this up, too." Deputy Leckie raised the gas can he'd retrieved with a gloved hand. "It appears to have some fingerprint smudges on it."

"Good!" Sheriff Jackson cheered. "Where did you find it?"

"The suspect dropped it as I advanced on his position—"

"Great news!" Sheriff Jackson nodded. "Maybe, we can lift some fingerprints off the darn thing and run that license plate down, too."

"Hopefully," the deputy said, "I will bag this gas can and log it into the Evidence Room right away, and we'll be able to get it over to Columbia on Monday. They have the best fingerprint lab in the state."

"Do that, and get that partial license plate over to dispatch for them to run it down."

"Sure thing."

"Thanks for your good work here tonight, Leckie," the sheriff said, retracting his former position. "If it wasn't for your vigilance, this whole church might've gone up in flames. But as it stands, the fire chief says they think they can keep the damage contained to the Fellowship Hall."

"That is good." The deputy shrugged. "But, indeed, I hate it had to happen at all—"

"Me, too!" The sheriff pounded an angry fist into his palm. "This is not good. This is not good for The Presidents. This is not good for Screamer. This is not good for Nolan County. And *this* is not at all good for our department!"

CHAPTER 19

"We are sick, sick, sick to death over what happened to your church, Pastor Strong," Pastor Renfrow said at their closed-door meeting in his office on the Saturday morning following the fire at Mount Olive. His round table was always a welcomed place of refuge to share with his fellow disciples. "And we've just got to stop meeting like this!"

"Indeed!" Bishop Pride said, echoing his heartfelt concern. "This can't keep happening. What're we going to do—"

"We…are going to move on in the name of the Lord!" Pastor Shaundra Strong said, her charming face resolute and undaunted. "'When the enemy shall come in like a flood, the Spirit of the Lord shall lift up a standard against him,'" she said, strengthening her resolve by reciting her favorite passage from Isaiah 59:19. "And we've got to do our part, too, pastors," she said, "by standing in faith and solidarity with the Lord."

"Amen, my sister!" Pastor Renfrow said, catching the fire of her fervor.

"Well, it goes without saying that I'm onboard," Bishop Pride said. "Because of the love and generous spirit you've shown to Holy Ghost Headquarters, we're behind you all the way. Whatever you and the Mount Olive congregation decide to do, you have our full backing…both spiritually and financially."

"We sincerely appreciate your support, pastors, because this certainly is a trying time," Pastor Strong said. "Our challenges with blending our combined congregations…and, now, this. These hateful acts are putting a strain on the whole community—"

"You're right. The black and white folk in Screamer can't even look each other in the eye anymore."

"And The Presidents would've exploded last night—"

"Oh, my, yes!" Bishop Pride shook his head woefully. "The Presidents would've surely gone up in flames if Mount Olive had burned to the ground like Holy Ghost Headquarters."

"But thanks be to God, Deputy Leckie got to the scene on time."

"During these trying times," Pastor Renfrow said, "I guess it's our role to keep a brave face before our community, in order to keep them from losing their heads, until these evil malefactors can be caught and brought to justice."

"I don't know about that," Pastor Strong rebutted. "The more I think about it, it may be high time for The Presidents to come together and say, 'No more!'" Her troubled countenance displayed the wealth of her passion. "No more white cops putting their knees on our necks! No more shooting our young men in the back! No more fat cats bringing their drugs into our community and poisoning our kids! No more gangs and gun violence plaguing our streets! No more treating us like second-class citizens! No more white racists having the unmitigated gall to burn down our treasures!"

"All that you say needs to be addressed," Bishop Pride inserted, "but tempers are raging red hot right now, Pastor Strong, and they might get totally out of control if we were to add any more logs to the fire."

"I agree with your passion and sense of urgency as well." Pastor Renfrow offered her a solemn nod. "But I also agree with Bishop Pride's call for restraint. When our immediate crisis passes, the three of us can form a coalition to address all the issues plaguing The Presidents. We'll be strategic. We'll work with the community and do our level-best to make Screamer stand up, take notice, and bring about needed change. Agreed?"

"Okay." Pastor Strong's shoulders relaxed. "But we can't wait too long."

"Agreed," Bishop Pride said.

"In the meantime, if it meets with the approval of you both," Pastor Renfrow said, "I'd like to hold a prayer vigil, starting here tonight at Beulah Bible, and invite the entire community to attend. And whenever you're ready, we can alternate between Beulah Bible and Mount Olive to keep the prayer chain going."

"Yes," Bishop Pride agreed. "I think that's a great idea. The saints must keep praying to our Great God as we keep working together to bring His Kingdom agenda down to earth—"

"I agree wholeheartedly," Pastor Strong said, "but I'm also very grateful to the two of you for giving me the liberty to speak my mind here today. But, as you say, our self-control and solidarity at this time could very well be our salvation…and that of the people in The Presidents."

"Amen!"

****

On the Saturday following the botched fire at Mount Olive, the 4-G Crew was also holding a meeting. They were hunkered down in the private confines of their secluded spot near Nolan Lake. Since this was not a particularly happy occasion, however, there was no celebration—no food, no beer.

"What happened, Gus?" Greene growled. "What went wrong?"

"Don't start in on me!" Gus' thick lips tensed into a tight ball. "It wasn't you out there, Radio Man, taking all the heat and running for your life—"

"Enough!" Gabe flared. "We're not here to point fingers. We're here to figure out our next move."

"True."

"I understand the WNL was none too happy." Greg III fished for details.

"Of course, they weren't happy!" Gus flamed. "When I reached out to our unit prez last night, he didn't even wanna take my call—"

"What?" Greene's chubby face blazed. "What's up with that?"

"When I finally spoke with Clive, in the wee morning hours, he reminded me…and in no uncertain terms…that our mission is *in*-complete…and if we get caught…we're on our own—"

"Like we didn't know that already!"

"And I had to ditch the getaway car and burn it." Gus pouted. "That fool, Leckie, got a partial off the license plate—"

"Where did you burn it?" Greg III asked; after all, it was his money going up in flames.

"You don't need to know." Gus squinted in his direction. "But if we decide to move forward, you're gonna need to buy us a new one—"

"Oh—"

"And…there's another little problem," Gus said; his voice fading to a whisper.

"What?"

"I dropped the gas can—"

"You did what?!?"

"You left the gas can behind—"

"Were you wearing gloves?"

"No." Gus shrank. "I forgot. I left my gloves in the car…but I wasn't expecting to lose the blasted can, now was I?"

"Then…what're we gonna do?" Greene shrieked. "If they lift your fingerprints—"

"I know." Gus squatted down on the lowest rung of the picnic table. "Don't you think I know? My fingerprints are on file at the Sheriff's Office—"

"Then, what's the plan?" Greg III paced a tight circle, hands wringing. "We can't get caught! What would they do to us? What would happen to the mill—"

"I can see you're just coming from the mill," Gabe said, trying to stave off his pal's mounting hysteria, "and you're looking mighty dapper, my friend." Greg III was wearing a fine tailored suit while the other three were dressed in scraggy shorts and tees.

“Oh-h…you mean, the suit…on a Saturday?” Greg III slowed his pacing to catch up with his thoughts. “Well, I just made company president…and I have to dress accordingly…and I know my daddy will absolutely kill me if we get caught!”

“Then, we’d better not get caught…and we’d better be glad it’s the weekend!” Gus hopped off the picnic table with an inkling of an idea. “They won’t be able to get that gas can over to the main fingerprint lab in Columbia ‘til Monday. And that means…we’ve got to get it back into our hands today!” Gus trotted toward his pickup. “And Greene…you’ve gotta help me! C’mon! Let’s ride!”

CHAPTER 20

It was later that Saturday afternoon when Gus and Greene came face-to-face with the unsuspecting property clerk in the Evidence Room at Sheriff's Headquarters in Screamer. The two of them had plotted their strategy on the ride over in Gus' pickup. When they finally skidded through the door, the twice-decorated Sergeant J. D. Gillum was on shift behind the check-in counter.

"Hey, there, Sarge!" Chief Deputy Gus McVey greeted warmly. "Do you know who this is?" he said, pointing to his 4-G buddy, *Radio Man*, Greene Jones.

"Do I?" the sergeant said with a beaming grin. "Of course, I know that man. That's the voice of Friday night football under the lights at Screamer High…in the flesh!"

"I am indeed!" Greene's fat jowls rocked jovially as he pumped hands with the sworn officer of the law. "I'm your man!"

"I need to check on one of my cases," Gus said to the clerk. "Won't take but a minute—"

"Just as long as you sign the roster first," the sergeant said, "no exceptions." But he was too enamored with the presence of *Radio Man* to notice that Gus was carrying a duffle bag into the Evidence Room. In accordance with departmental regulations, it was a practice expressly forbidden, but Gus was dragging his bag low to the floor so it couldn't be seen.

"While I'm in here," Gus said with a wide grin, "I'll leave you two to figure out a better strategy for our Mighty Tiger's offensive line. Screamer High's new head coach sure could use your help—"

"Yes, indeedy!" Greene added heartily, distracting the officer's attention away from the unlawful duffle. "The Tiger's offense sure has been sagging a bit of late, but I'll bet you and me can figure it out, Sarge…lickety-split."

With that, the two men at the counter put their heads together, and Chief Deputy Gus McVey slid into the Evidence Room. He removed the gas can that undoubtedly bore his fingerprints, and he replaced it with an identical can that was as clean as a whistle. Gus stuffed the accusatory gas can into his low-slung duffle and eased it out of the room.

"Well, did you two guys figure it all out?" Gus chortled upon his return to the counter.

"Back so soon?" Greene grinned, trying to establish the brevity of time Gus had spent in the Evidence Room in case he ever needed an alibi. "Well, Sarge, I guess we'll have to take this up when we've got more time, but it has truly been a pleasure talking Tiger football with you!"

"Well, anytime," the sergeant said, grinning from ear to ear. "It's always a pleasure to get a chance to talk to the voice of WSCR radio." As the sergeant was waving his fond farewell, Gus had handed off the unlawful duffle to Greene, and they both whistled their way out of Sheriff's Headquarters with the convicting gas can in their desperate clutches.

****

It was nearly dusk when Gus and Greene made a bee-line from the Evidence Room at Sheriff's Headquarters to their secret hideout by Nolan Lake. They reunited with the rest of the 4-G Crew who'd been anxiously awaiting their return.

"We got it!" Greene hoisted the hefty duffle that contained the convicting gas can. "We did it!"

"Good news!" Greg III sagged with a heavy sigh of relief. "I was beginning to worry—"

"No worries, Money Man," Gus said, "we've got everything under control. I burned the car where no one will find it; that blasted license plate is somewhere at the bottom of Nolan Lake; and we've retrieved the gas can with my fingerprints—"

"Perfecto!" Greene lifted the duffle again, backing his partner's play. "Gus' plan to steal this little piece of incriminating evidence worked like a charm."

"How'd you do it?" Greg III pressed for details.

"Gus and I rolled up on the property clerk at the desk, acting all chummy-like," Greene said, puffing out his rotund belly. "And while I was charming the poor guy out of his socks, Gus went into the Evidence Room; traded out the gas cans; and came rolling back out like nothing ever happened." Greene added a polished chuckle. "*Presto-Change-o-Alakazam*...I was carrying out the duffle with the contraband gas can, and the property clerk was left looking like a boob—"

"So...the WNL doesn't have a thing to worry about, and I told our unit prez just that on our way back over here," Gus said.

"And what did Clive have to say for himself?" Gabe asked. "What's the WNL's take on things?"

"Well, they've got mixed feelings," Gus said.

"But why?"

"They were truly excited by the first fire—"

"But—"

"But that's ancient history to them as you'd well imagine," Gus said, attempting to sound optimistic. "You know how it is with these guys. It's always: 'What have you done for me lately.' And it's their opinion that a botched church fire won't get Jackson kicked out of the Sheriff's Office—"

"Then, what do they want?"

"They want what we want!" Gus blared. "They want that black's badge!"

"Then, what're we gonna do?"

"We've gotta burn that last church…down to the ground!" Gus scrubbed his blonde head with a tight fist.

"And just how will we do that with everyone on such tight vigil—"

"I don't know just yet," Gus said, "but I've got myself a few ideas—"

"What? What?"

"Now's not the time!" Gus raised a stern hand to quiet his buddies' concerns. "But take it from me, we will get the job done. We will run that black joker out of Nolan County—"

"But why can't we talk about it now?"

"There're some things I need to get done first—" Gus pushed back.

"Like what?"

"Like buy a new getaway car with your cash, Money Man," Gus said, mussing his friend's slick, black hair. "And you've gotta get your DNA test done—"

"Oh, that's right." Greg III nodded. "I can really get on that now…since I finally made president at my daddy's mill—"

"Yeah, Greg III, man, you made president!" The other 4-Gs shared a hearty belly laugh. "We heard you the first time!"

"And after we've completed our mission," Greene said, ribbing him in the side, "we'll take the time to really celebrate your rad accomplishment…you can count on it!".

"Yes! Real soon!" They all circled Greg III in the bond of true brotherhood, and he was thrilled beyond words to be totally accepted by his only friends—for life. *Rad!*

CHAPTER 21

Even though she was totally oblivious of her husband's secret meetings and nefarious plans with his 4-G Crew, on the Monday after the botched church fire, the *Preacher-Man's* wife, Molly Anne Pritchard Ingram, was planning a private meeting of her own. She didn't come announced. She just took a chance that Cora Lee Jackson would be at her home on Jefferson Street at the end of her afternoon shift in the Screamer High cafeteria. Molly dressed as inconspicuously as she possibly could. Given the unrest in the black community after the two unfortunate church fires that had been spiritedly reported in the *Screamer Times*—along with the not-so-subtle warning that it wasn't safe for a white person to be caught in The Presidents—she thought it best to be careful. In spite of all the risks, however, Molly prayed; summoned her courage; and drove her unwashed Nissan coupe to The Presidents. As she bumped across the railroad tracks, she wondered if she'd ever been on that side of town. *No, I guess not. I guess I never had any reason to come down here before.*

Molly parked her vehicle carefully at the curb at the address Betsy had reluctantly supplied. She got out; locked her doors; and took faltering steps up the walkway to Cora's house. She didn't know what she'd expected on the black side of town, but it wasn't the tiny, run-down, wooden structures that dotted the landscape throughout The Presidents. After tripping onto the raw concrete porch, Molly gave a slight knock on the worn front door. There was no answer. Molly knocked a bit louder the next time. Still no answer, but she waited. Her heart was in her mouth, and her feet were firmly planted on the spot. In the palm of her sweaty left hand, Molly was clutching the plain, brown manilla envelope that Betsy had given her. Her mismatched eyes were fluttering, blazing—on full alert. Her faith in God's perfect plan had always helped her stand-up to the bullying and meanness from the cool kids at Screamer High. *Now, Lord, please give me the faith to accept the reasons why.*

"Molly Anne?!?" You could've bought Cora Lee Jackson for a nickel when she opened the front door to find her standing there. "What're you doing down here, child?" Cora's soulful brown eyes showered the young woman with a wave of compassion and deep concern.

"Hi, Miss Cora—" Molly said, displaying the same amount of respect she'd always tendered her at Screamer High. Her troubled eyes were swirling with color, and her free hand was fiddling with her kinky, blonde ponytail. "May I…may I come in?"

"No," Cora said, glancing back at the clutter and dreariness of her tiny living room. "I'll come out," she said. It's a nice day. We can sit together on the porch—"

"Fine—"

"Can I get you something to drink?"

"No, ma'am, thank you," Molly said, finding her tongue and her manners.

"What brings you down here?" Cora broke the deathly silence as they assumed their places in the worn metal chairs on her sparse front porch. For a few heartbeats, they both gazed vacantly at the school kids playing on Jefferson Street.

"My mommy gave this to me," Molly said, pressing the plain, brown manilla envelope into Cora's hands. It was moistened by her sweat.

"What is it?" Cora said as she emptied the envelope of its contents. "Me? A younger me, of course…standing over there in front of Beulah Bible." The creases on Cora's tired face blossomed into a warm smile. "Beulah Bible's the one that's got that famous floor-to-ceiling window with the beautiful, stained-glass cross—"

"It's a picture of my mother…my birth mother." Molly quickly brought her to the point. "She told me—"

"What would make Betsy Pritchard go and tell you a thing like that?" Cora gaped, stunned by the revelation. "She promised me she'd never tell you—"

"But I'm pregnant!" Molly cried and sheltered her belly with the palms of her loving hands; although, her baby bump was barely noticeable.

"Oh?"

"And Mommy told me for fear the baby will come out looking like you…black—"

"Oh!"

"Why did you just dump me?" The very words that had haunted Molly since the day she'd known were spilling out of her soul, like the wealth of tears that were flowing from her mismatched eyes.

"But I couldn't keep you," Cora said softly; her brown eyes were moistened with a weight of guilt and concern. She was having to face a truth she'd tried so very hard to bury. "I couldn't bring a white baby into my mamma's house. And I couldn't tell my family…I'd been…raped. It would've killed 'em. And I didn't know how I would treat you…knowing that I was—"

"Where were you attacked?"

"At a church…at this very church…the one right here in this picture." The photograph was trembling in Cora's worn hands.

"You were raped…in a church?" Molly said with a touch more sympathy.

"Yes." Cora sniffed. "It was an un-holy act in a holy place—"

"But how…in a church?"

"I was trying to make a little extra money during Spring Break…over at Beulah Bible," Cora said, breathing heavily. "I was in college back then; you know…and I was taking extra-special care to clean that beautiful, stained-glass window with the shining cross…it was always my favorite. I loved the way the sun shined through it from the outside and made it sparkle on the inside…all over the choir loft, the pulpit, and the pastor. When you were sitting in the pews, it was like a magical light show. That blessed cross showered in a rainbow of colors all over the sanctuary every Sunday." Cora shifted uncomfortably in her metal chair. "In order to do it justice, I'd get up on a little stepladder so I could reach it all the way to the very top. It was like a ritual for me. I'd gather my cleaning supplies; get the ladder; and sing 'Jesus Keep Me Near the Cross' while I cleaned every inch of that beautiful window, but—"

"What?" Molly prodded. "What?"

"As I was focusing on my task," Cora said in a whisper, "a man tipped over my ladder. I hadn't seen him come in. He must've snuck in through the side door that I forgot to lock. But before I knew what had hit me, the man rammed his knee into my belly and pinned me down to the floor in the choir loft. He stuck his hand up my skirt and—" Cora gasped for air and struggled to breath.

"It's alright. It's alright." Molly stopped her. "You don't have to say any more."

"I don't know if he came in there to burgle the church or just ransack it for meanness," Cora said, picking up the fragile threads of her painful memories, "'cause that white man had no business being in Beulah Bible on a Saturday morning—"

"Then, what did you do?"

"I couldn't move for what seemed like forever," Cora whispered. "But I finally mustered up the strength to roll over and get up on my feet. I didn't think. I couldn't. I just pulled my clothes together as best as I could; picked up the ladder and cleaning supplies; and I put them back in the janitor's closet. I went into the women's restroom, but I couldn't stand to see myself in the mirror. I just wadded…my panties into a ball…and I tossed 'em in the trash. Somehow, I made my way home." Cora's body gently rocked in her old metal chair. "I remember crying to myself all the way, 'Why, me, God? Why me? I ain't never done nothing to nobody.'"

"Did you blame God?"

"For a while, I guess, I did…but not anymore," Cora replied thoughtfully. "God gives us all a free will, and our sinful acts against one another are of our own choosing…not His. Besides, what we have to go through in this life is a testimony that God is stronger than whatever the world sends to break us." Cora tensed. "But...then again…I ain't never been able to go back up into that choir loft—"

"Well, did you at least go to the authorities?"

"I didn't even tell my own brother, Bertram Jackson. He was the first black deputy in the Sheriff's office back then, and I didn't wanna cause him no trouble on his new job." Cora breathed. "Besides, wasn't no white men gonna take no black girl's side in Screamer, South Carolina. They're more KKK in these parts than you know; especially, Sheriff Magpie and his crooked bunch. Besides, according to my granddaddy, lynching black folk is how Screamer got its name—"

"So…you just got rid of me—"

"I didn't abort you like I could have—"

"Oh, my!" Molly cringed at the sharpness of Cora's words.

"But…I want you to know…I never really wanted to do that," Cora said, in an attempt to soften her bluntness. Afterall, her views were shaped by the harsh realities of black life in The Presidents, while her child was living uptown in the sheltered world of white privilege. "Besides," Cora said with a touch of gentleness, "Betsy Pritchard was a preacher's wife, and she promised me if my baby came out white, she'd protect it and love it like it was her very own—"

"And if it came out black—"

"Well, she had some of her other rich friends, ones who weren't too hung-up on color, lined up to take it—"

"But I'm not an *it*!" Molly squawked. "I'm Molly Anne—"

"Yes, Anne…named after my mama…Anne Sukie Jackson—"

"Your mom?"

"Yes, my mama works right out there at that Allen Mills to this day. My daddy, Leo Jackson, was already dead. And when the son took over Allen Mills, Mr. Greg II, he made a big push for Affirmative Action for black folk and women. And my mama had just gotten hired on…and…if I had tried telling Sheriff Magpie what had happened to me, my mama might've lost that good job—"

"Then, you just abandoned me to Betsy Sue Pritchard—"

"No, I didn't abandon you!" Cora's eyes dipped to a crack in the old porch floor. "I looked out for you as best as I could. That's why I took that nothing job at the school's cafeteria so I could keep a close eye on you when you came of age. I've got two years of college; you know. Back then, maybe, I could've got me a good job out there at that Allen Mills—"

"Then, why didn't you?"

"It's lots o' things I never got to do after that. I never graduated college. I never got married…never had me no more children." Cora's brown eyes softened to console the look of sadness that was overwhelming Molly's mismatched eyes. "But…I…I have loved you…I've loved you hard…all of your life…because you're my one and only…but I had to keep my distance so I could protect you—"

"Protect me?" Molly's repressed anger betrayed her. "Well, I don't *feel* very protected right about now—"

"But—"

"And I'm too ashamed to tell my husband…my daddy…and my church—" Molly whined like a two-year old. "I'm so afraid what they may think of me…what they might do when they find out. What am I going to do? What am I supposed to do—"

"You wanna keep the baby?"

"Of course, I want to keep my baby." Molly's butterscotch eye scorched into the woman she now knew to be her birth mother. "I'm not like you. Gabe and I are married, and we want lots of babies—"

"Then, you're gonna have to come clean…tell the truth—"

"Tell the truth!" Molly's tortured eyes flamed. "Who ever told me the truth?!?"

"I understand your shock, and I understand your anger." Cora tried to console her daughter in her own special, matter-of-fact way. She still had a hearty zest for life despite her many disappointments. "But after you've had time to come to terms with it all, you've gotta see it for what it is," Cora whispered. "It is what it is—"

"Is that your answer?" Molly clapped back angrily. "It is what it is?!?"

"Baby, that's what I had to do…and with Jesus' help I've been able to deal with what happened to me." Cora extended her brown hand to gently pat Molly's white one. "I ain't hating on that white man that raped me no mo'…I don't wanna kill myself no mo'—"

"Kill yourself?"

"Yes, baby," Cora said quietly. "I didn't only consider killing you; I considered killing myself, too. But I'm happy the Lord stood with me instead, and He's giving me the pleasure of looking upon your lovely face today…and I can finally speak the truth—"

"What truth?" Molly whimpered, sounding as weak as a lost kitten.

"Now, at long last—" Cora's warm hands gently caressed her daughter's cold ones. "I'm able to say to you…I'm your mother, Molly Anne, and you're my one and only baby girl—"

"Oh-h!" Molly's bi-colored eyes bled tears. "And I do thank you, too, Miss Cora…for letting me live and not die…for giving me the chance to be here today…and for giving me the chance to have my own babies—"

"Shush, now, child," her mother said. And, finally, Cora Lee Jackson had the privilege of doing what she'd been so long denied. She leaned in and rocked her white baby girl against her pounding brown chest on her natty little porch on Jefferson Street in The Presidents.

CHAPTER 22

"Gabe, are you busy?" Molly said, entering her husband's home office/man cave behind a timid knock. It had been two days since she'd met with Miss Cora Lee Jackson, and she'd prayed her heart out until she'd finally gotten up her nerve. *Lord, please fix Gabe's heart to give me the kind of favor that Queen Esther received from her beloved King Ahasuerus.*

"Never too busy for you," Gabe said, smiling. He stopped what he was doing to give his wife his full attention. "Sorry, we haven't had much time to spend together lately, baby…been so busy with the church…that new Trustee Trainee Class—"

"Oh, I know." Molly's troubled eyes were rolling like a stormy night. This was the day she'd planned to tell him the truth—the whole truth and nothing but the truth—and she was praying that her telling eyes wouldn't betray her fear and misery. "Just wanted to talk to you about something…something important."

"Oh? What's that." Gabe sat up taller in his desk chair as Molly approached.

"Wait…who's that?" Molly said when she saw the picture of the man lying on Gabe's desk. She didn't quite know how to broach the subject that had been boggling her mind for days, so she was grasping at straws to delay the inevitable.

"That, my dear," Gabe said with a glowing smile, "that is Gus McVey's long, lost daddy—"

"Oh?"

"Remember me telling you back in school how wigged-out Gus was about not knowing his daddy?"

"Yes, I remember." Molly nodded. "Back then, it was a real big deal for him."

"Still is…or was," Gabe said. "Sit down, baby…have I got a story to tell you."

"And when you're done," Molly said, clutching the plain, brown manilla envelope she held in her clammy hands, "I've got a story to tell you, too."

"Deal," Gabe said, and he began to tell Molly the story of Gus' quest to locate his dad. Gabe told her about Gus finding the picture of the white man in his mother's things; how the man was in the criminal database; how Gus had secretly tested his DNA against the man's and found it to be a match.

"So…Gus' daddy is a criminal?' Molly's mismatched eyes crossed.

"Yes, a real bad guy," Gabe said. "He was even sent to the electric chair—"

"Wow! What in the world did he do?"

"They called him The Shutter-Bug Rapist—"

"The what?" Molly's eyes twirled like multi-colored lights. "He raped women—"

"And…he killed at least one of them—"

"How did they know? How did they catch him—"

"Don't exactly know, but seems that he kept a scrapbook of himself at the scene of every one of his crimes. He didn't try to conceal his identity from his victims. He just used the element of surprise to overwhelm them—"

"Then, his victims were able to identify him?"

"Yep, a few of them came forward…and they found his scrapbook with eleven pictures of him at crime scenes, but at least one more picture appeared to be missing—"

"Wow!" Molly's eyes puzzled. "After all that, Gus is still happy that *this* man is his dad?" Molly flopped the picture back onto Gabe's desk like it was contaminated.

"Happy as a clam." Gabe shrugged. "He's just happy the guy is white—"

"Hmm—" Molly said, and her mismatched eyes dipped to the floor like a meteor.

"What's the matter, babe." Gabe came around the desk and bear-hugged his wife. "I sure hope my telling you about Gus' gruesome discovery didn't upset you."

"It's not that—" Molly stuttered. "It's just that I have something very important to tell you, too, and I don't know where to start."

"Start at the beginning," Gabe said and took a seat beside his wife. "You can tell me anything; you know that."

"You know…I was adopted."

"Yes, of course—"

"And I've never really tried to find my birth mom."

"Yes, I know—"

"But now—" The envelope in Molly's hands was shaking violently. "I know."

"You do?"

"Yes." Molly's eyes twirled like bright-colored saucers, and she handed over the envelope to Gabe that she'd been squeezing so desperately.

"What's this?"

"Just look inside."

"Oka-y." Gabe lingered over the photograph. "Hmm…it looks vaguely like…*The Lunchroom Lady*…a much younger version of course…but, yes, it's her." He eyeballed his wife. "Right? It's the Lunchroom Lady."

"Well—" Molly breathed deeply, straining for clarity. "That's Miss Cora Lee Jackson…and…well…she is my birth mother—"

"What?" Gabe felt faint. He felt betrayed. He felt confused. He felt sick to his stomach to think what his 4-G Crew would say when they found out that his own wife's mother was a black woman. But he also felt a ton of remorse for his hidden feelings and for the tragic look that was overwhelming his wife's troubled eyes. "Oh, honey," he finally said after regaining his voice, "how did this happen?"

"It started back when Mommy was involved with the Right-to-Life Movement." Molly braced up in her chair, and she told her husband the whole sorted story of how Betsy Pritchard was barren and just had to have her own child. "Mommy met Miss Cora at the abortion clinic. And she was there because…because she'd been raped—"

"Raped?!?"

"Yes—" Molly faltered to gather her thoughts. Gabe's startled response was making her feel even more afraid. "And she…she was raped by a white man—"

"And Betsy came to her aid—"

"Yes."

"So…you've spoken with Miss Cora?"

"Yes."

"And what did she have to say for herself?"

"She feels like she didn't have any choice but to give me up for adoption. She couldn't just show up at her parents' house with a white baby; now, could she?"

"Then why didn't she go to the cops—"

"You know the folks down in The Presidents never trusted Sheriff Magpie—"

"Well, who did?"

"And Miss Cora says she took the cafeteria job at Screamer High so she could keep a close eye on me when I came of age."

"I…I just don't know what to say, Molly." Gabe slumped in his chair. "This is all so—"

"Bizarre." Molly finished his thought.

"Ye-s," Gabe stammered, "and you believe her…you believe Miss Cora?"

"Oh, Gabe, everything she said rang true." Molly's eyes regained their luster. "Gabe, she even *feels* like my mother."

"Oh—" Gabe quit speaking and gathered his beloved into his arms and just squeezed.

"Oh, Gabe!"

"Then, does Mike know?"

"No, Mommy never told Daddy…or our church—"

"Well, I guess everybody's got secrets—"

"Huh?"

"Oh, nothing." Gabe breathed. "Then, you're worried about how your daddy and the church will feel when they find out you're not all white…half black…half white…mixed…whatever—"

"No," Molly said in a quiet tone, "I'm only concerned about how *you* feel—"

"I love you, Molly Anne Pritchard Ingram," Gabe said quickly and unequivocally. "You're like a piece of my own soul. We can't do a thing about what happened before you were born, but, now, you…and only you…have my heart—"

"Oh, Gabe!" Molly collapsed into his embrace, and he flooded her with warm kisses. "I've been so, so worried that you'd reject me…hate me…even leave me—"

"Never!"

"Then, what're we going to do?" Molly sighed. "How can I lay all this on my daddy…the church—"

"I don't know," Gabe said, speaking from his assistant pastor's hat. "But the truth is the truth…and it will certainly put their faith and love to the test—"

"That's for sure." Molly released a nervous giggle. "But as long as I have your love and support, Gabe, I think I can face anything."

"Good." Gabe sat Molly up in her chair and tenderly wiped the tears from her mismatched eyes. "I guess your heritage is like your eyes." He smiled. "One color for each of them."

"Guess so." Molly returned his smile and laid the picture of The Lunchroom Lady on his desk beside that of Gus McVey's long-lost dad.

"But wait one minute!" Gabe said, being the first to make the discovery. "Look at these two pictures. They've got the exact same background."

"Yes." Molly caught on quickly. "Miss Cora said her picture was taken in front of Beulah Bible in The Presidents—"

"So…why was this picture of Gus' white daddy taken in front of a black church in the exact same spot—"

"You're right!" Molly gaped. "Look, you can't miss it…that floor-to-ceiling window…adorned with that brilliant, stained-glass cross. The crosses are identical!"

"You don't think—"

"Could it be?" Molly collapsed on Gabe for support.

"Gus said his dad took a picture of himself at the scene of every rape," Gabe said. "Do you think this could be the missing twelfth picture from his scrapbook of horrors—"

"Oh, my, Gabe—" Molly's eyes ran the circuit—from brown to blue and back again. "Do you think this white man…this…this vile rapist…could possibly be…*my* daddy, too?"

"I…I don't know—"

"Well, I've got to know!" Molly pressed her husband. "I've just got to know—"

"Maybe, I could get Gus to run another DNA test," Gabe said. *But what will Gus and the other 4-Gs say when they find out that my own wife…isn't a full-blooded, purebred white woman?*

"I've got to know—"

"I understand—"

"No, you don't understand." Molly's brown eye burned into her husband like love on fire, and the blue one kissed him like a cool caress. "It's not just for me I've got to know—"

"What're you saying?" Gabe frowned; his nagging doubts were trying to get the better of him.

"Gabe…I'm pregnant." A faint smile eked from the corners of Molly's lips. "We…are pregnant—"

"Whoo-hoo!" Gabe lifted his wife off her feet and twirled her around the room. Just those few words had erased all of his concerns and doubts. "We're pregnant! We're pregnant—"

"And after all this, you're still excited?" Molly said, pounding his arms to put her down. "Even if that vile rapist...Gus' long-lost daddy...turns out to be my long-lost daddy, too?"

"Honey, there's nothing...nothing in this whole, wide world that could keep me from being excited about having a baby with the woman I love!"

CHAPTER 23

"Gabe, what in the world are you doing here?" Gus buzzed angrily from the confines of his desk in the Sheriff's Office. He was second-in-command to Sheriff Jackson, and like their rank, their office doors sat side by side. "We shouldn't be seen together here," Gus said in a tight whisper. "You know that—"

"But—"

"Besides, I've got enough heat on my tail this morning—"

"What's the matter, Gus?" Gabe whispered. "Why're you so upset?

"Come with me." Gus put a heavy hand on his pal's shoulder and pushed him along the corridor. "Let's talk outside."

"What's the matter, Gus?" Gabe asked when they reached the parking lot. "I have never seen you so nervous in my entire life—"

"You'd be nervous, too," Gus said, "if there was a full-scale, in-depth investigation blowing up your skirt—"

"About what?

"About what happened to a certain *missing* gas can—"

"But how do they know it's missing?" Gabe caught his drift and lowered his volume. "I thought you'd replaced it with an identical can—"

"I did, Preacher Man," Gus said in a spiteful whisper, "but we're deputies and investigating is what we do. Besides, that li'l black snot shot off his mouth—"

"What li'l black snot…the desk clerk?"

"Naw! He's white as milk and no more the wiser—"

"Then who?"

"You should've heard him at roll call this morning—"

"Who? Who?"

"That blasted Deputy Leckie, that's who!"

"What did he say?"

"He said, 'I swear to you, Sheriff Jackson, on the eyes of me dear mother, there were fingerprints on that gas can I handed over to the Property Clerk,'" Gus said, mimicking Deputy Leckie's Geechee-born accent. "He told Jackson that he'd seen smudges on the gas can with his own eyes, and it should be a break in the case to bring the *bad mon* to justice who set the fires at Holy Ghost Headquarters and Mount Olive."

"And what did you say?"

"Nothing." Gus' thick lips set into their familiar sneer. "I just sat there like the rest of the white officers…acting like that black is as cuckoo as he looks—"

"So…what now?"

"Now…they're looking all over for that missing gas can," Gus said. "It all hit the fan on Monday when the lab in Columbia reported that there were absolutely no fingerprints or smudges on that piece of evidence we'd sent—"

"Maybe, you should've left some smudges on it—"

"Maybe…in hindsight…but who knew?" Gus waved his hands furiously. "There're so many loose ends…and now you show up here…looking all suspicious…and making me look suspicious—"

"You're overacting, Gus," Gabe said. "There are any number of reasons why the Assistant Pastor from the highly-respected Church of the Evangelicals might show up on your doorstep. Calm down!"

"I am calm." Gus jammed his hands into the front pockets of his uniform. "I'm just scared to death that they'll check the Property Clerk's log; find my name; and then put two-and-two together—"

"That's only in your mind, Gus! There is absolutely no way for them to be able to pin this on you…a lot of deputies go in and out of that Evidence Room—"

"You're right. You're right." Gus exhaled in one shallow breath. "Then, what does bring you down to my workplace on such a fair-weather day?"

"Well, seeing as how you're so upset, I guess I'll cut right to the chase—"

"Please do," Gus growled, "I've gotta get back in there and keep a sharp eye on things."

"I have a favor to ask—"

"Shoot!"

"There's this woman at our church," Gabe said with a shrug, "and…well…she was raped some years ago…by a white man—"

"And you want to know if that white man was my daddy." Gus quickly filled in the blanks.

"Well, yes," Gabe said, "and she's married—"

"And she didn't tell her husband she was raped—"

"Right!" Gabe said, weaving his story. "But this woman had a baby after the rape, and she doesn't know if it's her husband's—"

"Or the rapist's—"

"Right." Gabe nodded. "And I've been counseling the woman for years for depression, but her condition isn't getting any better—"

"And you think she would get better if you could put her mind at ease about the man who raped her…and who is the father of her child—"

"Man, Gus, you are a mighty quick study today." Gabe feigned a chuckle.

"Yeah, man, I should be. I've had some of those same thoughts myself—"

"What?"

"I wonder…I wonder did he rape my mother, too?"

"Who? Your dad?"

"Yes—"

"Probably not," Gabe said, "otherwise, he wouldn't have given her one of his trophy pictures from his prized scrapbook. Maybe, after he got with your mom…and knew you were on the way…he just wanted her to have something to remember him by—"

"Maybe." Gus scrubbed his blonde head. "Yeah, that makes sense."

"So…you can understand why this woman I'm counseling needs answers. She needs to get her child's DNA tested—"

"Well, I don't know—"

"What do you mean you don't know?" Gabe pressed. "You got your DNA tested against the guy and found out he was your dad—"

"Yes, and that's why I can't do it again—"

"But why not?"

"I had to squeeze that favor out of the lab tech as it was…and I promised him I wouldn't do it again," Gus said. "It's against the law to run the private tests; you know. That fellow could lose his job—"

"But it's just this once more, Gus—"

"I don't know—"

"Please, Gus. This woman is at her wit's end, and I shutter to think what she might do to herself if she can't bring closure to what happened to her so many years ago—"

"Then, what are you gonna do for me?" Gus twirled his lips into a wicked grin.

"Do? What?"

"Well, I'm ready to move on—" Gus checked around him to be sure there were no looky-loos or listening ears. "I'm ready to move on with the final straw in our mission…if you know what I mean—"

"Yes, I know," the Preacher Man said, "the last church—"

"Yes." Gus nodded. "And I sense I might get some pushback from—" Gus checked around them again. "From our other pals—"

"I understand…Greene and Greg III—"

"Yes." Gus snapped a quick nod. "So…if I can get your word that you'll back me to move forward, I may give this DNA test thing another go—"

"You will?"

"If you will—"

"Yes, I will," Gabe said, committing to back Gus' play with the other members of the 4-G Crew.

"Then, I'll see what I can do with my lab tech buddy." Gus sneered. "Besides, the guy owes me a big-time favor for a Screamer High football bet...maybe I can parlay that into at least one more of these off-the-book tests—"

"Get it done," Gabe said. He handed him the DNA sample that he just happened to bring along in a tiny, brown paper bag. "And I'll keep my word; I'll back you one hundred—"

"Consider it done!" Gus pocketed the DNA sample and headed back into the Sheriff's Office. "And don't you ever come back here again!"

"I hear ya!" Gabe waved his hand overhead as he walked away.

****

But it had been on that previous Sunday night—before Sheriff Jackson realized that the gas can in his possession was a fake—that he and Lucille had indulged in what could be classified as a *spirited* debate in the privacy of their own master bedroom about the growing racial tensions in Screamer.

"But, honey," Sheriff Jackson said, resisting his wife's intense cross-examination, "we *are* making progress."

"How so?" Lucille questioned, crossing her long, lean legs from the perch of her plush vanity chair. "You haven't caught the person or persons unknown who burned down Holy Ghost Headquarters and tried to do the same to Mount Olive—"

"I know," Sheriff Jackson said, "but this time we've got some real evidence—"

"Oh? What?"

"Lucille, you know I don't like talking sheriff's business with you—"

"You can tell me, honey." Lucille solemnly raised her right hand. "I'm on your side, and I promise…I won't tell another living soul—"

"Okay," her husband said, "but this time, you cannot tell anyone—"

"Okay…I said I promise—" Lucille rolled her eyes in his direction and flicked back her blonde-streaked tresses.

"Well, okay." Sheriff Jackson squared his broad shoulders. "The arsonist accidently dropped the gas can at the scene of the Mount Olive fire—"

"That's good, right?"

"Yes, if we can find some fingerprints on it, and the crime lab in Columbia will be doing the test first thing tomorrow morning—"

"Why's it taking so long—"

"It's the weekend, honey, and they can't look at it before Monday—"

"Well, I'm sure finding a real suspect will be a big relief to the forced union between Bishop Pride and Pastor Shaundra Strong—"

"Yes, I've been very proud of the way they've come together to help each other in this trying season—"

"Yeah, but I'm surprised Pastor Shaundra ain't slapped the Bishop by now—"

"What do you mean?" the sheriff said, feigning ignorance to his wife's worldly way of thinking.

"You know; they ain't never got along." Lucille let out a rich belly laugh. "Everybody's all proud of 'em now, but if it wasn't for Pastor Renfrow, the Bishop would've run Pastor Shaundra out of town the minute her foot hit Screamer…a woman pastor!"

"I know; you're right…and maybe…just maybe…the Lord's doing a roll call to see who's on His side—"

"Well, I know what side these kids in The Presidents are on—"

"Me, too, sad to say. They're angry. They're confused. And it's understandable—"

"But it ain't just these fires that's causing it." Lucille fluttered around the room in her royal red robe. "These kids ain't being raised right…fast mamas…run-around daddies…it's no wonder they're always mad as hell and ready to fight at the drop of a hat—"

"And it doesn't take much to ignite all of that hurt and disappointment—"

"We all come into this world stupid." Lucille fumed. "That's why we've gotta learn about Jesus and how this world really works…at home and at church…before we mess around and get it all twisted—"

"You're right; this world is definitely not our friend. In fact, it's out to destroy us," the sheriff said. "The only way we can make it is to follow Jesus. His truth and values are the only things that can guide us through the tough times in this life—"

"But without being taught, kids nowadays are disrespectful…to their parents; to their teachers; to their elders; to themselves." Lucille ticked off her complaints on her brilliantly-manicured nails. "And they refuse to go to church where they can learn that they *are* somebody—"

"Yes, we are all very special to Jesus—"

"But these kids aren't being taught to run behind Jesus…who can give them life." Lucille waved her arms in desperation. "No, sir, they're running behind these folks on TV and social media who don't give a flying-flip whether they live or die—"

"But Jesus proved His love. He died for every one of us on that cross—"

"But these kids don't wanna hear 'bout no Jesus, Bertram. They wanna hear what these rich white folks got to say. They hold them up as the gold standard. They hold them up higher than God." Lucille fluttered. "They want everything these white folk's got, and they want it now—

"But they must *position* themselves to get it—"

"Pray for it—"

"Go to school for it—"

"Work for it—"

"Before they can ever really succeed—"

"But no-o…they want these white folks to love 'em…and give it to 'em." Lucille rocked her neck. "But that ain't never gonna happen—"

"And it doesn't need to happen!" The sheriff bowed out his strong chest. "Because once you're a child of God, you've got all the love you'll ever need to make it in this cruel world. And the Lord gives us the strength to work for whatever we want—"

"And success does not come overnight." Lucille winked at her husband with a wry chuckle. "Look how long it took me to make you Sheriff of Nolan County—"

"Don't go there, Lucille!" The ex-deacon pinned his wife with a cautious eye. "This is God's world, and God is the source of all things…no matter what little part He allows us to play in it. Pastor Renfrow taught us that, remember?"

"I know all that, but I'm telling you the plain truth of it, Bertram," Lucille said. "These kids believe white folk are the source of all things—"

"Well, I guarantee you, they'll be sadly disappointed." Sheriff Jackson firmed his stance. "Because folk…all folk…will let you down. Look how there're coming after me…black and white…night and day. But God is not like man. He'll give you what you need. He'll help you…just like He's helping me deal with all these crazies in Screamer. The Lord is who we need—"

"I'll grant you; we're on our way to heaven, Bertram, but we ain't there yet. That's why we also need us some law and order." Lucille sniffed. "Look at how that white man just up and killed my daddy…for no good reason at all. And as long as evil white folk feel like they can do whatever they please, the law is all we've got to stop 'em from killing us. Black folk…all folk…have gotta feel like they can get some justice in this world, or they'll lose their minds and start taking matters into their own hands—"

"You're right, honey—"

"Black folk generally approach things from the heart," Lucille continued, without skipping a beat. "White folk generally look at things from the pocketbook. That's why we'll never see things eye-to-eye. We're never gonna find *common* ground. That's why it's up to the law to make sure we find *equal* ground—"

"But they're gonna try to hold onto their white privilege—"

"Of course, they are, Bertram…who wouldn't? Lucille shot her husband a sizzling glance. "But the law has got to make sure they don't use that *white privilege* to tap dance all over our heads. The law has got to keep the playing field level so that each of us has an equal opportunity to work for what we want. God gave *all* of us dominion over His world…but some folk are gonna want more than their share. That's why the law has to make sure we play fair so each of us has a chance to enjoy our own li'l piece—"

"You're right, Lucille; you're right," the sheriff said quickly before his wife could carry on with her preach "I'm the law, and we've gotta catch this blasted fire bug before—"

"Before he takes a swing at Beulah Bible." Lucille shook her head and pinned her husband with a jaundiced eye. "'Cause I can promise you, Bertram…if that church goes up in flames, all hell's gonna break loose down here in The Presidents!"

CHAPTER 24

"That spook, Jackson, has set up night patrols around every one of those black churches...and he's got that other one, that Assa Leckie, leading the patrols!" Chief Deputy Gus McVey raged at his 4-G Crew.

"So...what do we do now?" Greene's jaws flapped with concern.

"We do what we do!" Gus flamed. "Since we can't get to that Beulah Bible at night, we'll hit it during the day—"

"Oh, no! You're not thinking about going down there during the daytime—"

"But I have no other choice," Gus said, "because, by golly, I'm determined to get this done!"

"Talk some sense into him, Gabe," the others pled.

"Gus, it's not wise for you—" But before Gabe could fully frame his objections, Gus paraded a white envelope under his nose. Having a whiff of the answer he so desperately sought, Gabe did a swift about-face and said, "But I'll support Gus in whatever he decides."

"Wh-at?!?"

"That's right!" Gus cheered; and seeing that Gabe had kept his end of the bargain, he handed him the sealed, white envelope along with a wicked wink.

"Well, then, when will you do it?" Greene threw up his hands in disgust.

"Next Saturday afternoon."

"Well, now, in the spirit of full disclosure," Gabe said, stuffing the sealed envelope into his back pocket. What he had to say was tough enough, and he wasn't ready to tackle the surprises that the envelope might hold. "I've got something I need to tell you, fellas."

Gabe braced his foot against the picnic bench for support. "So…get ready—"

"What?" The remainder of the 4-Gs gave him their undivided attention. Whenever he got to sounding like the Preacher Man, they always listened.

"I don't know how to say this—"

"Say it! Say it!"

"My wife, Molly…well…she found her birth mother—"

"She did?"

"And…her birth mother…well…she's The Lunchroom Lady—"

"The who?" The others sank onto the picnic table.

"*The*…Lunchroom Lady!"

"You're kidding, right?" Greene's eyes bugged out. "But that's a black woman!"

"I told you not to marry that girl, remember?" Gus' face blew up like a hot-air balloon. "With those crazy, mismatched eyes and that kinky, blonde hair—"

"Hold on there!" Gabe's foot hit the dirt. "That's my wife you're talking about—"

"Right!" Gus yelped. "And, now, you're telling us…she's half spook!"

"She didn't know!" Gabe returned the heat. "She didn't know until just here recently when Betsy Pritchard told her the truth. We all knew she was adopted, but Betsy didn't even tell her husband that Molly's birth mother is black—"

"So…now that you know," Gus said cagily, "what're you gonna do about it?"

"Do?" Gabe looked at him like he was sprouting horns. "What would you suggest I do?"

"Get rid of that half-breed as fast as you can!"

"She's my wife!" Gabe's foot stomped the ground. "And I love her like my own life. That's not gonna happen—"

"Then, how can you call yourself a true white brother?" Greene piled on.

"Right!" Gus steamed. "How can you?"

"I am a true white man." Gabe held his ground. "I'm a true white man…married…to a woman of mixed race…that's all—"

"Which by definition," Greene said, "makes you so-oo not a true white brother—"

"Right!" Gus agreed.

"Well, say what you want," Gabe said, "I'm married to Molly, and we're gonna stay married. And not only that, my beautiful wife is expecting our first child—"

"Wh-at?!?"

"Oh, no! Oh, no!" Gus scrubbed his blonde head with a raging fist. "What're we gonna do?"

"And why're you so quiet over there, Money Man, huh?" Greene nudged him to join the fight. "You need to jump right in here with the rest of your white brothers—"

"But…but I can't," Greg III said, blue eyes dragging the ground. "I…I really can't—"

"And why not?" Gus raged.

"Because—" Greg III pulled a letter out of his jacket pocket and spread it onto the picnic table. "You see…I did my DNA test…just like you asked me to, Gus, and here're the results." Greg III pointed, and the remainder of the 4-G Crew gathered around the table with great interest.

"So what?" Greene questioned. "It says here that 50% of your DNA shows Eastern European…just like ours—"

"And 10% is other—"

"But what is this 40%?" Gus frowned. "It says…Nigerian and Congo—"

"Isn't that in Africa?" Greene gaped.

"Yes-s," Greg III stammered. "It says nearly half of my gene pool comes from…Africa—"

"That means you're a nig—"

"Don't say it! Please, don't say it!" Greg III begged. He slicked back his black hair, and his cloudy blue eyes fluttered aimlessly.

There was an intense silence alongside Nolan Lake. It was like the sound of Christopher Columbus' Santa Maria colliding with the slave ship La Amistad—somewhere deep in the Middle Passage—and the 4-G Crew were its 21st Century casualties.

"Well…I guess what they say is true—" Gus' snarly words broke the trance to find their mark.

"What?"

"All racists ain't white!" Gus said spitefully, but his attempt at sarcasm flopped like a cow's tail.

"So…your daddy's been *passing* all this time?" Greene threw down the gauntlet. "How do you think people in this town would feel…if they knew the CEO of Allen Mills…is a real, live…spook?"

"No!" Greg III's blue eyes filled with giant tears. "It can't be! Oh…but I really don't know!"

"Then, don't you think you need to find out—"

"I haven't spoken to my dad about this yet." Greg III swiped away his frothy tears. "He's been in the hospital; you know…it's his heart—"

"We know—"

"And I didn't want to upset him—"

"Upset him?" Gus' thick lips curled into a snarl. "Seems like it's a lot too late for that."

"But I will…speak to him about it, I mean," Greg III said in a faint whisper. "This is just all too hard to imagine…that all these years…me…me thinking I was a white man…looking white…acting white…being white—"

"Yeah-yeah!" Gus chanted an irritated sing-song. "Well, your daddy should've told ya!"

"So…what are we going to do?" Greene looked to Gus.

"Well, Radio Man, looks like we're the last two white guys standing—"

"Yep." Greene gave his pal a crisp nod.

"Then, it's up to you and me to complete our mission—"

"You think we should?" Greene's jaws dropped.

"Well, I know you've been tainted by all this, Gabe," Gus said, turning to him with a look of full-blown disgust, "but do you think you could do us this one last favor—"

"*Last* favor?" Gabe frowned.

"Well, yeah!" Gus flamed. "Surely, you don't think the WNL will let you go to the main compound or meet the Grand Master after this, do you?"

"Well—"

"And, Money Man, you've already served your purpose." Gus gagged out the words, refusing to even look in his direction. His long-time friend was now one of the most hated species in the world—a black man—and having to look at his black hair would only remind Gus of his true heritage. "I've already bought a new getaway car with your cash; I've got a stolen license plate that can't be traced back to us; and I bought Greene all the burner phones he needs to make the fake calls. *You*, on the other hand, need to go tend to your sick daddy…and get the details of your shameful birth—"

"But Gus—" Greg III's knees nearly buckled under his sharp rebuke.

"*Dis-missed!*" Gus blared. "You will never get the chance to meet the Grand Master!"

"That's right!" Greene took his stand alongside Gus.

"So…Gabe, can me and Greene count on you for this one last favor…for old times' sake?"

"What?" Gabe's whole body felt queasy.

"Make sure Jackson is in one of your Trustee Training Classes next Saturday afternoon…and I don't care if it's his last one."

"Yes, I can do that." Gabe sagged, sounding like a whipped pup. Suddenly, he realized this signaled the end of the 4-G Crew. The rock-solid friendship he'd built his life on—the one he'd thought would never fail him and never die—was crumbling right before his eyes. He felt like the ground had been snatched from under his feet. His soul felt violated, and his tortured heart was in freefall.

"By the way, how's Jackson doing in that class?" Gus sneered.

"Better than expected." Gabe sucked in a broken breath. "He's really holding his own—"

"Feature that!" Gus mocked. "One of you jigaboos…good with numbers—"

"Yeah!" Greene ran his fat eyes over Gabe and Greg III. "One of *your* kind!"

"From here on out, we don't need you two half-breeds hanging around us," Gus said. "When that last black church goes up in flames on Saturday, they'll be kicking Jackson out of Nolan County before nightfall!"

"Yes-indeedy!" Greene cheered. "And I'll get the chance to play our favorite song this one last time…'A Mighty Fortress Is Our God'…jazzy style."

"Right-o, Radio Man, and we'll be invited up to meet the Grand Master at the main compound!" Gus locked arms with Greene, and they turned their backs on their former pals. Together, they erected an inviolate stone wall.

The unthinkable had happened. Gabe and Greg III had been summarily banished from their beloved 4-G Crew. Like hollow shadows of themselves, the two outcasts drug their way to their respective vehicles. Without looking back, they departed from their infamous hideout at Nolan Lake—for the very last time.

CHAPTER 25

When he drove away from the 4-G Crew's hideout for the final time, Gabe took a turn around Nolan Lake to pull himself together. According to Gus and Greene—the only purebred white men in their crew—he was no longer a member of the 4-Gs, and that thought weighed heavily on his mind. He was beginning to feel like his whole life was one big lie. As he circled the lake, there were brief moments when he'd even considered throwing himself into its watery depths to drown his troubles, but something within wouldn't allow the thought to take hold. Instead, he set out for home. During the long drive, Gabe was tempted many times to open the sealed, white envelope that Gus had provided, but he couldn't bring himself to do it. He'd had enough bad news for one day. When he finally arrived home, beaten and bedraggled, Gabe entrusted the sealed envelope into the hands of his beloved Molly.

"What's this?" Molly accepted his offering with a smile. "Your will?"

"No." Gabe sulked. "Why would you say a thing like that—"

"Gabe, lighten up!" Molly chuckled, twirling her kinky, blonde ponytail. "I was just kidding…but this must be serious—"

"Just open it."

"O-kay." Molly went into Gabe's home office/man cave to retrieve a letter opener, and then she returned to the living room and took a seat beside her husband on the sofa. "This really must be important." She sliced open the envelope and carefully read its contents.

"What does it say?" Gabe moved to the edge of his seat.

"It says—" Molly could barely form the words. "It says that that vile rapist…George McManus…is…my sperm donor." For the life of her, Molly couldn't locate the word *father* in her vocabulary, and she was loath to consider the implications that this discovery would have for herself and her unborn baby. "This is awful!" Molly's eyes juggled like balls of confusion. "This is the worse news…ever!"

"It is awful." Gabe drew his wife into his weary arms and found ways to comfort her. "But baby, we can't argue with DNA. It's the truth—"

"Then some truth isn't worth having—"

"No!" Gabe said, feeling the enormous weight of all of the day's harsh disclosures. "All truth is worth having, Molly. It just depends on what we do with it."

"Then, what do you suggest I do with this truth!" Molly yelped. "You want me to go around telling the world that I come from the seed of a murderer like…*The Shutter Bug Rapist*?"

"No," Gabe said, "I want you to tell the world that you come from the good seed of *The Lunchroom Lady*…a woman who's done everything in her power to make sure you've had a good life—"

"Miss Cora!" Molly's bi-colored eyes finally emptied all of the tears she'd held there. "My mother…Cora Lee Jackson…she did try to protect me, didn't she Gabe?"

"Yes, she did, baby." Gabe squeezed his wife tighter, attempting to arrest her seizing tears. "Your mother…your birth mother…did all she could under the circumstances."

"I'm having to reorient my whole way of thinking about myself and my identity, Gabe." Molly's mismatched eyes flashed the colors of the rainbow. "I feel dizzy. I feel like I'm floating…adrift. But my one constant…my rock…the one thing that will not move…is my knowing that I'm a child of God…and that will never change."

"Yup, even when life grabs us up by the toes and shakes us," Gabe said, speaking out of the wealth of his own personal pain, "the Lord is always right there to catch us before we fall."

The solemn couple was silent for a great while. They just held onto each other; loved on each other; and soothed the baby growing inside her belly. Finally, Molly found the words. "Gabe," she said, "you know what else this means, don't you?"

"Yes, Molly, I do," Gabe said, approaching the touchy subject with great reticence. "It means that Gus McVey is your brother—"

"Can you imagine that?" Molly's voice cracked. "That racist, Gus McVey, is going to find out that he has a half-sister…and she's half-black…ha!"

"I know you're upset, Molly, but don't be too hard on Gus. All of his life, he's been conflicted about his heritage. When the rest of us were satisfied with playing video games, he was worried if his daddy was white—"

"Then, it only serves him right," Molly said, "he gets a two-fer!"

"What's that?"

"A horrid white daddy who was sent to the electric chair…and a black sister as a bonus—"

"You don't mean that—"

"I mean it alright." Molly's voice cooled. "But my heart won't let me hate him…just feel sorry for him. But what will it do to poor Gus when he has to deal with this, too?"

"I don't know." Gabe firmed his back. "But like I said, the truth is the truth. All we can do is deal with it."

"So…how do you think Mommy will feel about all this? And Daddy…how're we going to tell my poor daddy?" Molly broke down into sobs again.

"Don't cry, baby." Gabe lovingly kissed her forehead. "It'll be alright. Your mom already knows that Miss Cora was raped by a white man; she just didn't know who—"

"Yes, that is right." Molly's mismatched eyes flooded hope for the first time.

"And my dear father-in-law, Senior Pastor Mike Pritchard, has seen lots of things during his long tenure in the ministry. I doubt if this will floor him—"

"You might be right, Gabe," Molly said, "Daddy is really, really strong."

"See! If we tell the truth…the whole truth…the Lord will help us sort all this out.

"You're right." Molly's blue eye sparkled, and the brown one danced.

"Which means—" Gabe fished for the words that gagged in his throat like drywall. "Which means…I've got to come clean, too—"

"You?!? Oh, no, Gabe, what have you done?" Molly's face creased with concern. "I don't think I could stand another horrible revelation tonight. Is it another woman?"

"Oh, no!" Gabe nearly chuckled. "I wish it were that simple—"

"Simple?"

"Molly—" Gabe sucked in a deep breath. "I've been leading a double life—"

"What?"

"Just hear me out—"

"Ok." Molly sat up bone straight on the couch, bracing for more bad news.

"You say, Gus is a racist." Gabe breathed. "Well, we all knew that back in school, and since he was our friend, we adopted some of his ways—"

"We?"

"The 4-G Crew."

"Oh?"

"And, over the years, we've been practicing our beliefs…by being members of a hate group…right here in Screamer—"

"No, Gabe! You!" Molly's bi-colored eyes startled. "You're a minister of the gospel. You teach the ways of love. You preach the ways of Christ every Sunday…every day. How could you?"

"It was easier than you'd think." Gabe dropped his head. "I guess I just compartmentalized. I care about you. I care about our family. I care about all white people in general—"

"But you're supposed to care about *all* people in general…just like Jesus—"

"I do…in principle. But as a practical matter, I guess I'm like a lot of other people. I care first and foremost about my own kind—"

"But your own kind are supposed to be Christians…all races, creeds, colors—"

"I know that, Molly." Gabe's jaws crackled. "Don't make this any harder on me than it already is—"

"Okay. Okay. I'm sorry." Molly's eyes mellowed to a precious hue of understanding.

"I do care about Christian people…all Christian people…the people we'll meet in heaven. But down here on earth…down here where the rubber meets the road…where there're good guys and bad guys…well, I want to be in league with the white guys."

"Then, you've been practicing racism, just like Gus and the other guys?"

"Pretty much."

"Then…how does that fit in with finding out that your wife is the daughter of a black mother and a white rapist?!?" Molly yelped while setting a tender hand over her baby bump.

"Frankly, it doesn't," Gabe said softly, attempting to contain the fallout. "I'm not trying to justify it. I just did it. And that's what makes it all so…so bizarre." Gabe was struggling to hold back his own tears. "But I do love you, Molly, with all of my heart…and I guess, somehow, love trumps everything—"

"Oh, Gabe." Molly's mismatched eyes lightened with the love in her heart for her husband, her family, and their unborn child. "I know you're a good man, and I love you, too. But how're you going to be able to continue along this path—"

"No!" Gabe stopped her short. "I'm done with all that! That's why I'm telling you about it now. I'm confessing it to you today…so I can ask your forgiveness…ask God's forgiveness—" Gabe finally broke down into bitter sobs.

"It's alright, Gabe." Molly rocked her husband tenderly. "I forgive you. I love you. But more importantly, God loves you, too. And, remember, Jesus already died for *all* of our sins, so we don't have to die for them, too…including this one—"

"Huh?"

"Remember, what the Bible says, Gabe? 'If we confess our sins, He's faithful and just to forgive us our sins and cleanse us from all unrighteousness,'" Molly said, quoting the Apostle James.

"But how can God forgive us for all we've done—"

"He can. He does—"

"But, Molly, you just don't know all we've done—"

"And I don't need to know!" Molly stopped him cold. "Whatever you've done was forgiven when you confessed it to Jesus, and I can't go behind that seal."

"Oh, Molly Anne Pritchard Ingram, you're such a fantastic woman!"

"A fantastic woman with a fantastic husband." She burned a sweet kiss onto Gabe's hot cheek. "And we never have to speak of this again—"

"But we've got to tell your folks…and Gus—"

"Well, my parents really only need to know how Gus and I are related…nothing more," Molly said. "And I'm very sure you'll do everything in your power to rectify the rest."

"I will," Gabe pledged with a raised right hand. "And I can't wait for us to tell Gus," he said, giving his bride a cocky half-smile and a knowing wink, "to tell him…my dear wife...that you are his half-sister."

CHAPTER 26

Greg III was devastated by the time he reached the hospital on that Saturday morning—the same day Beulah Bible was scheduled to go up in flames. His nerves were humming from lack of sleep, and his back ached from the agonizing strain. For days, all he could think about was the last time the 4-G Crew had met together at Nolan Lake. Gus' spiteful words had gutted his insides, and he was sick of spirit; so much so, his work as president of the mill was starting to suffer. What hurt him most was the fact that Gus and Greene—his *purebred* white buddies—seemed not to care in the least that their friendship had been disbanded. It was like, in one fateful moment, all of their years together—all of their shared memories, their dreams, their confidences—had counted for less than nothing. *Even in my wildest dreams...I could never have imagined that anything could come between us. But, now, me and Gabe...poor Gabe...are left to deal with all of our problems...alone.*

Greg III had tried not to bring the news of his DNA test to his dad, but he couldn't deal with his unanswered questions any longer. He slunk into his dad's ICU room and took a seat. No other names appeared on the visitor's log out front, so Greg III figured his dad was as rested as possible. "Dad…Dad are you up for a little serious conversation?" Greg III sighed heavily. "I need to talk to you about something—"

"Talk? Why?" His dad coughed, and his blood pressure monitor spiked. "Is there something wrong at the mill, son? What is it?"

"No, Dad. Calm down." Greg III attempted to level his voice to the steady bleep of the monitor. "Everything is running smoothly at the mill. What I have to say is a little closer to home."

"What then?" his dad mumbled, straining to prop open his heavy, drug-induced eyelids.

"You know I hang with the 4-Gs—"

"Yes, to your grandmother's great chagrin—"

"Well, that's her problem, now isn't it?" Greg III clapped back. "Those were my friends."

"Yes." His dad struggled to concentrate. "Please, son, get on with it."

"Well, Gus wanted us all to have our DNA tested so we could chart our family trees—"

"Why would he want to do a thing like that?" His dad's monitor jumped. "Why—"

"Well, we did it, Dad…and I guess you know what I found—" Greg III curbed his words as soon as his eyes fell upon his dad. In just those few moments, the man appeared to have shrunk three sizes.

"Yes," his dad said wearily, "I know exactly what you found. What I've tried to keep you from finding all these years—"

"The guys think you've been…*passing*—"

"*Passing*? I'm not passing…my dear son, you already know our family history—"

"Then, why, Dad? Why didn't you tell me?" Greg III's tortured voice plead earnestly. "Was it for fear of Grandmother Elsie?"

"Partly…I…I guess," his dad sputtered, attempting to pace his breathing. "But partly because I didn't want you to be saddled with it all of your life—"

"Saddled with what, Dad?" Greg III's voice spiked. "Saddled with—"

"Yes…saddled with knowing your mother…was a black woman, and saddled with how people in Screamer would feel about it…and how they'd treat you because of it—"

"But if you were ashamed of my mother, why did you marry her?" Greg III's voice did a swift rewind. "At least, I guess you married her…did you?"

"Yes, I married your mother when we were both in college at Columbia." His dad's breath quickened with every word. "She was from Macon, Georgia…she knew the risks. Seemed like the whole world was against us. But we fell in love…deeply in love. I never planned to come back to Screamer. I never planned to bring my lovely bride back to this hellhole…and around your grandmother—"

"But—"

"But Joy…your sweet mother's name is Joy Marie Madden. My beautiful Joy died giving birth to you…and I came back here…like it or not…because I needed your grandmother's help in raising you."

"Why didn't you at least tell me?"

"You…son…couldn't have handled it." His dad chocked out the words. "You're too weak…too insecure…look at the boys you call friends—"

"But, Dad—"

"Bring me…my briefcase. Do it…now—" his father instructed. "Look inside…my business cards."

"Okay." Greg III smoothed back his black hair, reset his glasses, and did as he was told.

"That…that is your mother, son." At the very back of his dad's business card holder was a picture of a woman, no bigger than the size of a half dollar. The woman had a slender caramel face and long, straight, jet-black hair; and she was smiling for the camera. But, undeniably, she was a black woman.

"This beautiful lady is my mother?" Greg III said, squeezing his daddy's hand. But, in that solitary moment, the heart monitor's beep went to a solid flatline, and his daddy drew his last jagged breath.

Greg III was lost. He stumbled through the cadre of doctors and nurses rushing with the crash cart to his father's aid, but he knew it was no good. He'd had to pry his hand from his daddy's death grip.

Solemnly, Greg III waited for the doctors to pronounce time of death, and then he fled like a fugitive from the confines of the sterile white walls.

****

When he was back at home on the Allen Estate, Greg III went straight to the big house. For this time, he didn't want to hide from his grandmother; he wanted to confront her. "Grandmother, where are you?" Greg III's voice resounded like a hollow echo in the grand foyer.

"Back here!" Elsie Louise Allen called out. "I'm in the game room." Greg III followed the sound of her voice, stopping in the doorway. "Well, don't just stand there like a moron," she said. "Come on in, boy! Come on in!"

"I'm afraid I have some very sad news, Grandmother." Greg III entered the room and took his usual seat across from the family's matriarch. "Daddy…well…my daddy died—"

"What?" Elsie felt faint. She had a tendency to wear too much red rouge and black eyeliner, and the lines and wrinkles on her white face were sagging into a comic mask. "What are you saying, boy? Speak up clearly so I can understand you!"

"Your son just died at the hospital."

"But how do you know?"

"I was there, and I came straight home to tell you—"

"You left him there alone?" Elsie said in bitter accusation. "You left my son there alone with strangers?"

"No, Grandmother." Greg III drew in a hot breath and released it. "I've made all of the necessary arrangements." Her doubting his ability to handle important family matters was resurfacing all of his ambivalent feelings toward this domineering old lady.

"Your father was my all-in-all…my rock." Elsie slumped. "I'm getting old and feeble, now, and without my beloved son, I don't know what I'll do." She fluttered around in her chair like a broken bird. "You're not your father's son by any means…but I guess I'll be forced to rely on you, now. I guess the two of us will have to pull together…like family—"

"Family?" Greg III spewed out a rye chuckle. "But do you know who the two of us really are—"

"Stop talking in riddles, boy." His grandmother stroked her scrawny chest. "You upset me when you do that…and I have enough to contend with right now. My son, my beloved son is gone…forever…and I'm left here alone with you—"

"I don't know if you'll want to be with me when you know who I really am, Grandmother Elsie—"

"There you go again, boy!" Elsie's hands slapped the game table, and her blue veins bounced. "I already know who you are. You're my son's only son. And as sorry as you may be…you're my only grandson—"

"No, Grandmother Elsie." Greg III proudly slicked back his jet-black hair, set aside his glasses, and burned his blue eyes into the woman who'd always made his life a living hell. "I'm not your only grandson. I'm your only *black* grandson…as black as the hair on my head—"

"What madness is this you say?" His grandmother gripped her heart, and her heavily rouged cheeks drooped down to her chin.

"I had a long talk with your son before he died, and he finally told me that my mother's name was Joy Marie Madden—"

"I know that—"

"But did you know, Grandmother, that my mother was a black woman—"

"No-o!"

"Did you ever see a picture of her?"

"No!" Elsie resisted the notion with two raised palms. "Your daddy said they never took pictures—"

"Well, here's a picture of my mother," Greg III said, and he rounded the game table to show off the prized photo to his grandmother.

"But this," Elsie stuttered through chattering false teeth, "this is a picture…a picture of a nig—"

"Don't you dare say it!" Greg III shouted. "That beautiful lady is my mother—"

"But your mother is a nig—" While the word was still forming in her mouth, Elsie Louise Allen slumped over in her favorite chair in her prized game room—never to be revived again.

Quickly, Greg III called in the butler to handle the 911 call for his grandmother because he had an even more urgent call to make. He was a black man, now, and he felt that he owed it to his roots—his mother—to stop Gus McVey from burning Beulah Bible down to the ground.

When he ran to his cottage, it was nearly 3 p.m. He called Gus on his cell. There was no answer. He dialed Greene at the radio station, and he finally picked up. "Greene!" Greg III yelped. "You've got to stop him! You've got to stop Gus from going ahead with his plans!"

"Don't know what business that is of yours, Greg III," Greene said coolly, "you're no longer a member of the 4-G Crew, remember? Besides, it's too late. Those burner phones you bought me have been buzzing all morning, and those deputies are having themselves one busy Saturday…hauling their tails all over Nolan County. And on top of that," Greene whispered furtively, "I've already had the pleasure of playing our favorite song…'A Mighty Fortress is our God'…jazzy style. Didn't you hear it? It's a go!"

"Oh, no!" Greg III dropped his phone and broke down in bitter tears in his little cottage behind the big house. "Daddy! Mother! Grandmother!" he wailed. He was sick to his very soul—no family; no friends; no hope for redemption. Lost and alone, Greg III finally granted his broken heart the gift he'd denied it for far too long—permission to grieve.

CHAPTER 27

Suddenly, Chief Deputy Gus McVey zoomed into Assistant Pastor Ingram's church office like a house on fire. His appearance was disheveled, and his white face had blossomed to a beet red.

"Gus, what's the matter?" Gabe jumped up from behind his desk to check on his recently-estranged friend; but before saying another word, he carefully surveyed the hallway and eased his door shut. "Sit down, Gus, and tell me what's wrong?"

"I…I can't—" Gus' brown eyes were bouncing around in his head, and he was stuttering like a shock victim.

"You can't what?" Gabe struggled to make sense of his buddy's giddy, dumbfounded expression.

"I can't sit." Gus paced the office like a caged tiger. "I can't sit…not until I tell you what happened to me, Gabe. You'll never believe what happened to me!"

"Ok-ay," Gabe said slowly, trying to settle his friend's keyed-up emotions. "Take your time and tell me what happened—"

"I…I—" Gus made tight turns on the plush carpet. "I—"

"Is it about the church fire?" Gabe coaxed. "Did…did something happen at the church?"

"I…well…yes—"

"Yes, what? Did you set the fire?"

"Yes…no—"

"Yes or no…which is it, Gus?"

"Okay-okay." Gus gave his nose a stiff swipe and reeled in his emotions. "I did. I went to the church—"

"And-and—"

"And I went to set the fire—"

"Did you?"

"I didn't get the chance—"

"Did someone spot you? Is someone following you? Is that why you're so upset?"

"Yes, Deputy Leckie spotted me…and he chased me—"

"Did he see your face?"

"No…at least I don't think so. I was wearing this." Gus shook off his black hoodie and ran a nervy hand through his matted, blonde hair. "But…but…you don't understand—"

"Gus, please make me understand," Gabe pled. "Sit down and make me understand."

"Okay." Gus accepted a seat at Gabe's desk, but his legs were still vibrating like a helicopter readying for flight.

"Okay, take it from the top," Gabe said, resuming his seat behind his desk. "Gather yourself, Gus, and tell me what happened…from the beginning."

"It all went down as planned." Gus' knees bounced furiously. "Greene made the fake calls to spread out the deputies. Then he played our favorite song on the radio—"

"A Mighty Fortress is our God—"

"Yup…jazzy style." A faint glimmer of a smile teased at the corners of Gus' thick lips. "And, then, I went to Beulah Bible with my equipment…to do the deed…you know—"

"To burn the church—"

"To the ground—"

"But—"

"But…I never got that far—"

"Deputy Leckie spotted you?

"No." Gus shook his head tightly. "No…not at first."

"Then what? What happened?"

"Okay." Gus wrapped his arms tightly across his chest to still his body. "As I got on my knees…to light the fire…under that prized cross…something happened—"

"What happened?"

"From out of nowhere, a beam of light burst through—"

"Through the cross?" Gabe shook his head. "But, Gus, that doesn't make sense. That's not possible. You were on the outside. How could the sun shine through the cross—"

"That's just it." Gus' body shook with renewed fervor. "I don't know…but all of a sudden the brightest light I've ever seen in my whole life came flaming through that cross…right into my eyes!"

"Wh-at?"

"It wasn't a normal light, Gabe." Gus' frame vibrated. "It was like a *body* of light…and all of it was shining…shining right down on me—"

"Then, what did you do?"

"I didn't know what to do. I tried to shake it off. I tried to get up off my knees. I tried to set the fire…but—"

"What?"

"Then, it happened, Gabe." Gus began sobbing like a small child. "It sounded like a single clap of thunder…a boom…louder than anything you could ever imagine. It did a fierce 360 degrees around the perimeter of the church. The fierce shaking started with me, and it ended with me…just me!"

"And what did you do?"

"I dropped the gas can. I just ran for my getaway car…and that's when Leckie spotted me—"

"Did he chase you?"

"Yes! First on foot, and then when I got to my getaway car, he gave chase in his patrol vehicle. He hit his sirens and blue-lighted me all the way through The Presidents—"

"Did he recognize you?"

"I don't think so." Gus tugged on his hoodie. "He chased me across the railroad tracks, but I finally lost him. I rammed my getaway car through that secret back alley; remember, that little, narrow slit we found as kids? Well, I ditched my car there, and I ran the rest of the way up the backside of the church to get to you, Gabe."

"Do you think Leckie will look for you here?"

"No. Why should he?" Gus puzzled. "Jackson just left here to go to the scene at Beulah Bible, right?"

"Oh, that's right." Gabe nodded. "We were in the Trustee Training Class when the sheriff got the call."

"But none of that's important, Gabe—"

"Not important? But you left the gas can behind—"

"No worries." Gus flipped his leather gloves out of the pocket of his hoodie. "I remembered to wear them this time…at the church and in the car—"

"So…what *is* important—"

"Don't you see!" Gus jumped up from his chair and nearly ran circles around the room. "Jesus shined that brilliant light through His cross right onto me, Gabe. And when that fierce clap of thunder made its loop, it not only shook the church to its foundation, but it shook me to mine as well." Gus slowed. "And while I was on my knees at the foot of that cross, I felt like anything was possible. I felt like I could be somebody…start over again…sins forgiven…past forgotten…even my rotten excuse for a daddy. I don't need anybody to validate me anymore because today…I met Jesus…and He found a way to let me know…He really does love me!"

"I guess it's possible it could happen to you," Gabe mumbled. "It certainly happened to the Apostle Paul on the Damascus Road—"

"I don't know this Paul fellow," Gus said innocently. "All I know is my eyes were opened today…maybe for the very first time. All these years you've been preaching this Jesus to me, but I didn't believe...not really. But, Gabe, I tell you, now, I do believe. That was no accident at that church today…no quirk of fate…no weird coincidence. In my heart, I had as good as burned that black church to the ground," Gus said. "But that beam of light didn't shine through the cross from the outside; it shined through the cross from the *inside*. And I don't know how to describe it, Gabe, but I *felt* it. I felt it down to my soul. I felt the power fall right on me!" Gus lifted up his hands in worship. "Jesus is alive, I tell you…and in that split second…I knew…Jesus really and truly is God!" Gus lowered his voice in reverence and said, "And if God can forgive me for all I've done…if God can love me…in spite of me…how can anyone else hold anything against me?"

For a long moment, the silence in the office was profound. Gus' words of faith had showered their hearts like fresh morning dew. Gus, who notoriously hated everybody—including himself—had professed His belief in Jesus Christ, and they were both awestruck.

When he was finally able, Gabe was the first to speak. "Human-love is about feelings in the moment, Gus," he said soberly, searching his friend's eyes for signs that he truly understood the gravity of his claims. "Jesus-love is about believing…knowing for a certainty that Jesus has already done for you everything that He's promised…everything you'll ever need…to live this life…and to take you to heaven."

"I know," Gus said humbly. "I believe."

"Then, are you saying you want to accept Jesus Christ as your personal Saviour?"

"I surely do." Gus' thick lips curled into a rare smile. "I am a true believer, now, and I want whatever He's got!"

"Then, okay." Gabe smiled and moved over to his bookcase to retrieve his Bible. "Let's see—" He turned to the Book of Romans, Chapter 10 and took a seat next to his longtime friend.

"What do I have to do?" Gus inquired.

"Do?" Gabe chuckled. "You've already done it. You've been converted. You've turned your heart from unbelief to belief. You've confessed Jesus Christ as your Lord. That's all it takes to be saved. But I do want to read this confirming passage of scripture, Gus, to give you full assurance of your faith before we pray."

"Okay."

Gabe read aloud, "'That if thou shall confess with thy mouth the Lord Jesus, and shalt believe in thine heart that God hath raised Him from the dead, thou shalt be saved. For with the heart man believeth unto righteousness, and with the mouth confession is made unto salvation.' That's verses nine and ten," Gabe explained, "but verse thirteen goes on to say it more plainly, 'For whosoever shall call upon the name of the Lord shall be saved.'"

"Then, I guess that's me," Gus chimed in cheerfully, "because I truly believe that Jesus Christ is Lord; and without a shadow of a doubt, He is alive and well."

"Then let's pray," Gabe said, and he did something he'd never done. He held hands with his friend, knee to knee, as they sat in that quiet place. "Dear Lord, I join with Gus, here, who has confessed You as Lord and Christ; and we thank You for saving Gus and me and making us Your own. And, Lord, we forgive all those who've mistreated us; and we ask You to forgive us for our sins, too…for the evil deeds we've done against Your people…and for the hate in our hearts that caused it. We ask you to remove it and to help us change our ways…and to walk in a way that is pleasing in Your sight. For, Lord, we realize that a changed heart is our only cure; and only You can change a heart. Please give us the Spirit of love that comes from You. It's in Your name, Lord Jesus, we pray. Amen."

Each of the men attempted to wipe the tears from their eyes before the prayer had ended but to no avail. They finally gave up on the attempt and just smiled at each other. "I feel like a load has been lifted off my shoulders," Gus confessed. "I've been dragging so much crap around all these years…my mother's drinking; all those men she slept with; the mystery of my birth. In fact, looking back, I think I picked black folk to hate just so I could have a place to put all of my rage—"

"I hear you, but all that's behind us now—"

"I'm not so sure." Gus sagged in his chair.

"Why? What's wrong?"

"The church fire—"

"But you didn't actually set the fire—"

"No…but my G-initial…the one that was on my keychain—" Gus gagged. "I think I lost it—"

"At the church?"

"I don't know…but when I was fumbling for my keys…I might've dropped it at the scene alongside the gas can—"

"Prints?"

"I doubt it. I had on my gloves, remember?"

"Then, it's no big deal—"

"Sure, it is." Gus scrubbed his blonde head with tight fists. "Because Deputy Leckie has seen my G-initial lots of times. He's even remarked about it, and he's the suspicious sort. If he finds it at the scene, he may be able to tie it back to me—"

"Don't worry." Gabe removed his own set of keys from his desk drawer. "Here, you can take mine. They're all identical, and I can get a replacement later. No one will suspect me. I've got an air-tight alibi—"

"Yeah, that's right." Gus gladly accepted the gift. "You were right here with Sheriff Jackson the whole time. Thanks, man."

"No worries, Gus." Gabe fist-bumped his chest. "We're *still* the Mighty 4-G Crew…to the end, right?"

"Maybe not to the WNL—"

"Uggh…why did you have to bring them up?" Gabe frowned. "I thought we tied all that off in our prayer—"

"Well, we did get an invite." Gus shot up from his chair and moved away from his friend. "As an incentive to get the last fire done, they invited the 4-G Crew to meet with the Grand Master at the main compound. You know I've always wanted to meet him, so I didn't let on that the fire had already been scheduled for today. But after the way our last meeting went down at the lake, I told our unit prez that you and Greg III were *otherwise engaged*." Gus shrugged and gave his friend a cheeky grin. "Sorry about that, man—"

"Oh, I understand—"

"But I did promise Clive that me and Greene would go; but after what I've seen today, I don't even know if we should—"

"Would it tie off loose ends for you with this WNL thing?"

"Bring closure, you mean?" Gus shrugged. "Sure."

"Then go…this one last time—"

"Do you think that's wise?"

"When any of us come to Christ, Gus, there're always some holdovers from our past…things we're not too proud of. But because of the Lord's grace and mercy, there're not to be feared; but, sometimes, they have to be faced."

"Thanks, Gabe, you always know what to do."

"And, oh, by the way," Gabe said with a twisted smile, "I think you probably need to sit back down."

"Why? What's wrong?"

"There's nothing wrong…but I've got to tell you about the results of that DNA test you ran for me."

"Oh, yeah, did that woman you're counseling find some peace?"

"Yes, she did."

"That's good…well, I guess," Gus said, resuming his seat as instructed.

"It's very good." Gabe slowly moved over to stand behind his friend's chair. "The DNA you had tested…well…it belonged to my wife…it was Molly's—"

"Molly?!?"

"And, Gus, I know you've never really cared for my wife…but the DNA test says…Molly Anne Pritchard Ingram…well…she's your half-sister—" Gabe was barely able to catch Gus before he hit the floor.

CHAPTER 28

It was finally the big night. Gus and Greene rode in Gus' black pickup, and they followed their unit prez and his young son to the main compound. Up, up they went from Screamer into the steep hill country near the North Carolina border. Since his recent conversion to faith in Christ and belief in the innate worth of all mankind, Gus' loyalties were somewhat torn, and his heart was racing. Greene was talking non-stop as was his own weird way when he was supremely nervous, but they took special note of every twist and turn toward their journey's end.

They parked their vehicles in a clearing alongside the others—cars, motorcycles, campers, and muscle trucks of all description. The night was dark. The forest was dense. Their tactical flashlights were casting eerie shadows along the narrow foot trail. The nocturnal serenade of cicadas, bull frogs, crickets, and screech owls was the only sound. It was all too creepy. Yet they followed Clive and his son on their silent trek to a campground in the middle of nowhere. For once, wearing combat boots as part of their standard gear made sense. Gus didn't know about Greene, but the strange surroundings were giving him flashbacks from some of his favorite black-and-white classic movies—the ones featuring illegal moonshine stills and determined Revenue Agents.

When they finally arrived at the main compound, it was pitch black except for lit torches that led the way to a quonset hut that was hidden under dense forest cover. There were armed guards standing at attention on either side of the entrance, and Gus and Greene were soaking up every detail. As newcomers, they were grilled and vetted before being allowed to enter with Clive and his son.

When they finally entered the poorly-lit enclosure, there were a host of white men dressed in fatigues, camouflage gear, and riot-styled helmets. Some of the fiercest-looking ones of the bunch had on blackout gear, and they were carrying some of the biggest guns Gus and Greene had ever seen. There was everything from AK-47s to rocket launchers evidenced around the room. The whole crazy scene made Gus' hair stand on end; but, tonight, he had to forget that he was the Chief Deputy Sheriff of Nolan County. Try as they might to appear cool, calm, and collected, however, Gus and Greene were extremely anxious; albeit, both of them were captivated by the electrically-charged atmosphere. And to top it off, they were deeply enamored with having the privilege of finally meeting the Grand Master—whom they'd worshipped from afar.

As they were ushered by Clive to the front of the room, his young son stepped back into the shadows. Following strict protocol, Gus and Greene took short, deliberate steps behind Clive to maintain themselves at his rear. Suddenly, the room dropped to a hush when they reached the massive desk that had been hewn from a mighty cedar. Behind the desk, the rear of a lone, high-backed chrome chair was facing the three men as they approached.

"Wait here, men," Clive ordered, and he left Gus and Greene standing at the front of the desk while he went behind to talk to the invisible man seated in the chair. Gus and Greene strained to hear what was being said.

"These are my two men who're handling our church fires," Clive whispered to the unseen presence. "They're thrilled with the opportunity to meet you tonight, sir. Will you do them the honor of an audience?" Clive fell back to stand beside his son amongst the waiting throng, and the chrome chair behind the mighty cedar desk slowly turned.

"You?!?" Gus and Greene gaped. "It's you?"

"Yes, boys, it's me," Ex-Sheriff Lester Magpie boomed, giving them a wicked wink. "I am the Grand Master of the illustrious White

Nationalist League and very proud of it. Why do you think we're backing you?" he said, leaning back on his regal throne. He had a slow, country way about him that gave off the mystique of supreme knowledge and great power. "We're determined to get that bumbling clown, Jackson, out o' my old seat for good. We want that black gone!" Magpie pounded his fists against his desk, and his attentive subjects saluted and screamed, "White Power!"

"You?!?" Gus repeated hotly. It was as if he'd meticulously followed the yellow brick road to see the *Wizard of Oz*, and he'd turned out to be this itty-bitty man with a big voice, hiding behind a fake wall of fear and secrecy. Gus was royally pissed, and in that split second, his eyes were enlightened. As he and Greene stood there, feeling like the boobs they were, Gus looked to his left and to his right at all the white faces hiding behind big guns, and he was enraged at the irony of it all.

"God made all men!" Gus fumed in righteous indignation. "But the only man that doesn't know the worth of the black man is the black man himself—"

"What!?! What did that fool say?" The nervy gallery rose to an unsteady roar, not believing what Gus had spouted in the midst of their sacred assembly; and they were eagerly awaiting the slightest signal from their fearless leader to go on the attack.

"We did everything in our power to kill off black folk during slavery…we beat some heads; we stole their identities; we split up families; and we strung 'em up…but we couldn't get the job done." Gus continued undaunted while Greene yanked on his buddy's elbow, fearing for their safety. But Gus' thick lips had set into a fierce snarl, and there was no stopping him now. He shook off Greene's best attempts and kept going.

"After the Civil War, poor white men…the ones who weren't wealthy, well-connected, or owned land…were just a step-up from being slaves themselves. And ever since then, we've been trying to prove that we may not be one of those rich, fat-cat white boys, but we are, indeed, better than any black man that ever lived. And we've been willing to burn, steal, and even kill blacks to prove it. We've been saying, 'I may not be rich, by-golly, but I'm white, and that makes me superior to any black any day!'" Gus pounded his chest like a wild man. "But there're poor folk in every race, and some of you in this room are as poor as Job's turkey. And we learned to hate black men because wealthy white men hated us, and we had to have somebody to hate to feel good about ourselves. And, oh, how *they* love for us to hate blacks, and they appeal to our lowest instincts to get the job done because it plays right into their greedy li'l hands. But, in your heart-of-hearts you know…these rich, fat-cat white boys wouldn't pour water on us if we were set on fire. And neither would these wicked politicians…like Magpie, here…who want to keep us on edge just so they can stay in power—"

"That's enough! I'll kill ya with my own bare hands!" Clive shouted as he pulled against his young son who was wrestling to restrain him. He was deeply embarrassed that these two turncoats were members of his fine unit. "I'm so very sorry, sir." Clive bowed to the Grand Master, and the crowd hissed its loud agreement. "Don't you worry! We'll get these traitors out o' here right away!"

"Naw! Naw!" The Grand Master leaned back on his throne, basking in the grandeur of his full authority. "Let 'em talk! Let 'em talk! We ain't in the mood to be killing no white boys here tonight." He puffed on his big cigar, and the tip seared with a hot blaze of fire. "Let 'em talk!"

"And you're out here playing like you care about the right-to-life…ha!" Gus continued, non-stop. "How could you care about life when you're willing to choke-out a black man with your knee on his neck; or shoot an unarmed black man in the back; or be willing to separate brown babies from their parents and put 'em in cages. You don't care about the right-to-life; you only care about keeping your fast-tail daughters from having abortions and killing off all our white babies!" Gus raged, undaunted by the beet-red faces of what was fast becoming an angry mob, screaming for his blood. "And you hate that your daughters are having babies by these black guys. Mixed babies, I might add, that you only claim as your own flesh and blood when you're pushing them around in your grocery carts at the Shop & Save—"

"Git him! Shut him up!" the assembly shouted, nearly coming uncorked, but Magpie signaled to his armed guards to hold back the raging hoard.

"Quiet down now!" Magpie blared. "I said these boys could say their piece here tonight 'cause this may be our last time seeing 'em...*ever* again—"

"Yeah! Right! String 'em up! Kill 'em!" the violent white men cheered.

"Don't get me wrong," Gus said, a little shook, but ever determined to get the heavy load off his chest. "I'm all for your ends, but you're going about it the wrong way. What you need to do is get your daughters into somebody's church so they can learn about the sanctity of life; of having good morals; and of respecting their own race. Let 'em learn something besides sex, drugs, and rock-n-roll, or who's *trending* on social media," Gus ranted. "We've gotta teach our children how to live with others...the way Jesus told us to...and, then, our supremacy...if indeed it does exist...it'll shine right through. But we can't just kill off everybody so we can be the last ones standing. Who do you think you are? Everybody's got a right to live...until God says different!" The tables had turned. Gus was speaking with the same fire of conviction he'd shown when he was planning to destroy God's churches simply because black people worshipped there. As Gus' vision sharpened, and he looked around the compound at all the other losers—losers like him, and Gabe, and Greene, and Greg III—losers who'd felt like the 4-G Crew when they'd been forced to be misfits at Screamer High—and, finally, he understood.

"And we stand here tonight," Gus said sadly as his eyes took in the room, "a bunch o' losers, hiding behind camouflage gear and big guns. You were willing to let us take the risk of burning down three black churches, but you wouldn't have backed us or defended us if your lives depended on it. You're out here in no-man's land, playing soldier and plotting your dirty, little games…ashamed to show your faces 'cause you don't want your employer, your wife, your friends, your families to know what disgusting li'l creatures you are.

"But don't get me wrong, I think it's commendable you want your sons to follow in your footsteps, but all the more reason you must be mighty careful where you're leading them. You've got your poor, young boys out here, indoctrinating them into this garbage at a time when they should be in somebody's church…in somebody's Sunday School class…learning about the love of God through Jesus Christ. But, no-o, you're willing to sacrifice your own children on the stinking altar of your false god of…*them-against-us*…which, by the way, is a myth you've manufactured in your own minds 'cause most black folk are just out there tending to their own business. But since you've been stockpiling all these weapons, you're willing to invent any excuse to use them." Gus swung his arms wildly around the room. "Now, take a real good look around you. Do you see any enemies here? Naw…it's just us…a bunch of white guys…talking tough…flashing weapons…and creating an atmosphere of fear for our kids." Gus slowly shook his head for the last time. "You are a sad bunch of misfits, trying to hide your impotence behind big guns, but you'd be scared to death if you ever had to use 'em. And for most of you, you'd pee your pants if any one of these black guys ever really came your way—"

"Grrrrr!!!" The assembly roared as one fierce man. "Git 'em! Kill 'em! String 'em up! Traitors!"

But Magpie held back their murderous intentions with one wave of his hand. "Silence!"

"But as for me and my 4-G Crew, we quit!" Gus turned and fist-bumped Greene, who was looking about ready to pee his pants. "For us, all the hate stops here...tonight. We don't need this, or you, to make us feel like we're important or brave. We don't need a Grand Master who hides out in the dark woods, and who'd turn his back on us at the first sign of trouble. We choose to live in the light," Gus said, shrugging off his deep disappointment. "The size of a man isn't determined by the color of his skin; or what he does for a living; or how much money he can stash away, but it's about who he is on the inside. And, now, I've got Jesus on the inside...and that's enough for me!"

Gus elbowed Greene that it was time for them to make a speedy exit. However, for a little added insurance, Gus unholstered the 45 pistol he had on his right hip and cocked it. Finally, Greene, who'd been paralyzed with fear until that very moment, summoned the courage to draw his pistol as well. As they slowly backed out of the compound, they kept their weapons pointed in the direction of the angry mob, discouraging any sneaky potshots. "And you need not worry about us telling *any-body* about the WNL," Gus yelled loud enough for them all to hear. "We would *never* admit knowing you bunch o' yahoos or the location of this demon-den of hate!"

"You don't tell! We don't tell!" the Grand Master yelled back in spiteful rebuke. "Because you boys are into this thang up to yo' necks. Don't you ever forget it...up to yo' necks!"

Once outside, Gus and Greene quickly retraced their steps down the wooded footpath, dodging the briers and dense underbrush as they fled. Finally, they jumped into their pickup and kicked it into gear. As they roared away, they were hoping Magpie wouldn't send any of his goons in hot pursuit. Fearing the worst, however, the two friends didn't dare breathe until they were back on the main road headed to Screamer.

"How did you know all that stuff, Gus?" Greene finally broke the tense silence. "In a way, I was really proud of you, dude."

"Dunno." Gus scratched his blonde head. "A documentary, maybe? But once I got started, it just flowed through me."

"You're serious about this Jesus-thing, huh?"

"I am," Gus confessed. "You ought to consider it, too—"

"Dunno." Greene looked out into the dark night sky. "Me and God aren't exactly on speaking terms; but if you believe, Gus, I'm certainly willing to listen."

"Well, that's enough for now," Gus said. And as they sped back southward, the light of a brand-new day began to dawn on the horizon.

CHAPTER 29

"So...you're my sister, huh?" Gus greeted Molly as soon as her foot touched down on their sacred hideaway at Nolan Lake. Gabe had driven his wife over to meet with the entire 4-G Crew in hopes of finally clearing the air and finding some common ground with Gus. Evening was approaching, and the sun was scrolling brilliant rings of magenta across the lake's gentle surface when they arrived.

"No...that would be your *half*-sister," Molly said directly as was her way. She settled herself onto the picnic bench and smoothed her dress over her growing baby bump.

"So...you've got one for each of 'em, huh?" Gus forced himself to gaze into Molly's mismatched eyes—one, a mossy brown; the other, a bright, shiny blue.

"Guess so," Molly said, returning his gaze without flinching. "They're my birthmark, and I'm proud of them."

"Does the preacher and his wife know?" Gus spat on the ground and scrubbed it out under his work boot.

"Mommy and Daddy? Know about you?" Molly's colorful eyes startled. "No...not yet...I wanted to talk to you first so I'd know what to tell them—"

"Why? What do you want from me?"

"Gus, ours is not a story worth telling," Molly said, "unless we decide, right here and right now, that we'll accept each other as family—"

"Family?" Gus pursed his thick lips and shook his head slowly and deliberately. "Hmm...you and me? I don't know about that—"

"What's the holdup, Gus?" Molly searched his eyes as the other 4-Gs looked on.

"Well, finding out you're my *half*-sister...well, that's been a shocker to say the least. And it's made me have to speak some very hard truths to some people I once worshipped—"

"But since you worship Jesus, now, that can't be a bad thing, can it?" Molly said softly.

"Well, it's made me have to take a hard look at myself and all of my motives...all the way back to childhood—"

"But having to take a hard look at ourselves...with the grace and mercy of Jesus on our side...that's not such a bad thing, is it?"

"But I'm having to recalibrate my whole way of thinking...about everything...how I stack up in the world...what I believe...who I am—"

"But if all this soul searching brings you closer to the truth, that can't really be a bad thing, can it?" Molly's mismatched eyes kept Gus under their steady gaze, and her kind voice never changed its pitch.

"She's making some good points, Gus," Greene chimed in. "You can't deny her logic."

"That's right!" Gabe and Greg III agreed, both totally amazed at Molly's handle on the situation.

"Besides, there's not a lot of difference between you and me, is there?" Molly persisted.

"I don't know—" Gus wavered and took a seat at the picnic table across from Molly.

"What difference?" The other 4-Gs rustled. "What?"

"Your mother's black; mine is white," Gus said, trying to explain away his reticence.

"But you have the *same* daddy," the 4-Gs carped in reply.

"Yes, the same low-life daddy," Gus said, "but is that enough to make us family?"

"It's enough...if we will let it be enough," Molly said, eyes level, voice steady, never skipping a beat.

"But how can you ever receive me as your family?" Gus' head drooped. "All the things I've thought about you and said about you...and the things I've done to black people—"

"But...but my mother's black, too!" Greg III's bleary blue eyes moistened with concern. "Gus, does that really make me any less your friend?"

"I sure hope not," Gus replied quietly, having given the matter some serious thought over a long, restless night, "because I've loved you like a brother my whole life—"

"And you still can," Greg III implored, smoothing back his black hair. "I...I haven't changed—"

"God made us all," Gabe said, and he took a seat alongside his bride. He warmly embraced Molly for the courage she'd shown, and he tenderly caressed her hands. "Nobody gets to pick their own race; we're born into it. Can we just start there and forget about all the rest?"

"Well, one thing's for sure," Gus admitted, "without knowing that Jesus loves me, I certainly wouldn't have been able to come here today—"

"Then, with Jesus, anything is possible, right?" Gabe reasoned.

"But...Molly...aren't you...ashamed of me?" The quiet words nearly gagged in Gus' throat.

"No," Molly said, "how can I be ashamed of you? You didn't have any more control over the circumstances of your birth than I did over mine." Her bi-colored eyes brimmed with unshed tears. "And I'm so willing to forgive you all the hurtful things you've ever said or done to me. You did them in ignorance—"

"Ignorance?" Gus bristled.

"Gus, ignorance is simply not knowing all the facts—"

"Oh—" Gus settled back down. "You're right...none of us had all the facts, did we Greg III?"

"No, we did not," Greg III said, breathing a sigh of relief. "And if we'll allow ourselves, we can let go of the past...and all of our parents' messed-up deeds and choices. We can start out fresh—"

"Yes!" Gus nodded vigorously. "I believe this family thing can work...but only better this time. Because this time, we can start out with the truth, and we'll let it take us wherever it takes us—"

"But we can't just fake it," Molly cautioned, "or play it by the numbers. Being family's not going to work unless we put some real love into it—"

"I can do love," Gus vowed, swallowing in Molly's questioning eyes. "Since I've met Jesus, I can do love. With Him in my life, I really do have love to give—"

"So...I'm your half-sister?" Molly's mismatched eyes mellowed to a hopeful hue.

"Nope, even better than that...you are my *sister*!" Gus moved in closer, and for the first time in their lives, he and Molly shared a warm embrace. "We can't do anything about the past, but I'm proud that my sister just happens to be my best friend's wife. And maybe, just maybe, I can get to be a godfather!" Gus' thick lips set into a beaming smile; and with the gentlest of hands, he caressed Molly's baby bump.

"Yesss!" Greene exclaimed, caught up in the tenderness of the moment. "We've spent entirely too much time trying to find reasons to hate and destroy." His fat jowls jiggled. "We were just trying to find somebody to hate...more than we hated ourselves. And we've spent too much time hiding in the shadows; hiding our true identities; and trying to get love out of people who never even gave a crap about us. Away with that!" he announced in his best disc jockey voice. "We've got each other, and we don't have to prove our worth to anybody...not ever again!"

In rapid succession, the 4-G Crew slapped down their matching G-initials onto the picnic table—side by side—as was their practice when they were in agreement. Gabe had purchased a replacement that was identical to the others, and Gus gave him a thankful nod. He was relieved that despite their misguided intentions and evil deeds, it seemed that they were all in the clear.

"And from this day forward," Gabe spoke for the four of them out of the depths of his heart, "we hereby swear…with Molly as our witness…that we will never meet at this spot to cook up mischief of any kind again—"

"We will keep the confidences of our past," Gus said, smiling knowingly at Gabe, "and move forward, together, as a family!"

"Yup! Agreed! We're all members of the same race…the human race…and the 4-G Crew is back together again!" Greg III looked to his beloved pals for confirmation. "Right?"

"All-for-one-and-one-for-all!" Greene heralded with his fat face beaming.

"Molly, your sweet spirit and your understanding has brought light where there was darkness this day." Gus' brown eyes softened. "And we are all truly grateful to you—"

"Here-Here!" They shared a laugh, slapped backs, and hugged Molly—their new mascot—until her feet were floating on air.

CHAPTER 30

Greg III's family had been among the founding members of The Church of the Evangelicals in Screamer, South Carolina. As such, each ensuing generation had been big-time tithers, but they hardly ever darkened the door. People gushed over them for their worldly accomplishments, but dead is dead. Each of us must go the way of all flesh; make preparations to meet our Maker; and arrangements to handle our remains. It was, therefore, only fitting and proper that Greg Allen II was put away in grand style on the grounds of the church's cemetery with his mother, Elsie Louise Allen, laid out alongside him in a twin coffin. The combined funeral service came as no surprise to anyone present. *Well, there she goes...that witch, Elsie Allen. Hmph! Everybody knew she couldn't survive without her darlin' son...but at least she found it somewhere in that cold heart o' hers to dote on that boy while he was yet living.*

But on the same day of the double funeral, in the confines of his French Provincial living room, Gabe and Molly told Senior Pastor Mike Pritchard the truth. His wife, Betsy, was in attendance, and she steadily nodded her assent to each one of the truths her husband was being told by Gabe—who even dropped the bombshell about how Molly and Gus were related. Mike Pritchard listened intently and without interruption. He neither made reckless accusations against his wife, nor did he level any reprisals against Gabe or Molly. Maybe, just maybe, it was because Mike Pritchard had been carrying a secret of his own.

As startling as the revelations appeared to be, Senior Pastor Mike Pritchard already knew. Even though the fact that George McManus aka The Shutter Bug Rapist was both Gus' and Molly's birth dad had come as a bit of a shock, Mike already knew that Cora Lee Jackson was Molly's birth mother. Back when Betsy had been acting so crazy about the adoption, Mike had hired a private detective to bring him a report on his wife's movements. It had vaguely crossed his mind that she might've been having an affair. Although with all his heart, he'd hoped it wasn't true; but he had to know. Consequently, he knew about Miss Cora—and the rape. He knew all about Betsy's undercover adoption. And despite all he knew, Mike Pritchard was delighted to have been given the privilege of raising Molly Anne as his very own baby girl. Despite her mismatched eyes and kinky, blonde hair, he had always considered her a precious gift from God; especially since the first time he saw her, she'd grabbed hold of his heart as tightly as she'd held onto his finger, and she'd never let go.

"So…that's the whole story, Mike," Gabe said as he ended his monologue and took a seat next to Molly. "We're all so very sorry we withheld these facts from you, but, now, we're giving you full disclosure as we know it."

"And I appreciate that" is all Mike Pritchard would say. He rose up from his favorite armchair and went to sit beside his wife on the couch. "I don't know if you need to hear this, Betsy," Mike said to his wife as he embraced her, "but I love you, and I forgive you all. I'm so glad you saw fit to bring our beautiful daughter into our home."

"Oh, thank you, Mike. I did need to hear that," Betsy said, flowering again. "I'm done. I'm done trying to make family…trying to hold things together…trying to make things come out the way I think they should. I accept God's will in the matter because only He has the power to hold things together." Betsy embraced her beloved husband. "And, Mike, I make you this solemn promise…I will never, ever go behind your back again—"

"And I love you both," Molly said, leaving her husband's side to encircle her loving arms around the only parents she'd ever known. "I don't care how I got here; I'm just glad I got here because you two are the best parents in the whole, wide world." Gabe joined the trio, and the four of them became real family that day—no pretense; no guilt; no secrets; no lies.

****

On the very next Sunday, dressed in his finest gold-trimmed burgundy robe, Senior Pastor Mike Pritchard mounted the pulpit at The Church of the Evangelicals. His wife, Betsy, was perched in her normal seat on the front row, lovingly eyeing her husband in what she considered to be his finest hour.

"There's something I need to tell the church this morning," the senior pastor said. "Something that I've known for some time, but I think it only fair to tell you now."

"Huh?!?" The 800-seat sanctuary skidded to a full stop.

"Our beloved, adopted daughter…our Molly Anne…is of mixed heritage—"

"Wh-at?!?" The tightly-packed sanctuary was an explosion of *oohs* and *ahhs*.

"I didn't know until recently how it *all* came about," the preacher went on to say, "but I want you to know that none of that really matters…none of that matters to me, to my wife, to my family…and I hope, if God is your witness, none of it will matter to you."

"Um-hmm—" The preacher's bold statement was met with a smattering of reckless eyeballs and a trickle of grudging *amens*.

"With that said, I have the distinct pleasure this blessed morning of introducing to our congregation a fine woman." Mike Pritchard's round face was glowing. "Many of you already know her because she's served faithfully in the cafeteria at Screamer High for many years…and if you have not had the privilege of meeting her, trust me, your children know and love her intimately."

A few weak chuckles scattered about the sanctuary.

"Please stand, Miss Cora," the preacher requested, and she did so obediently. "This, saints, is Miss Cora Lee Jackson, and she's with her mother this morning whom you may not know, Mrs. Anne Sukie Jackson, who works right out there at Allen Mills. And they are here this morning with one of our newer members and his wife, Sheriff Bertram and Lucille Jackson." Of course, Lucille was dressed to the nines. She stood up gracefully and gave a practiced princess wave to the wide-eyed congregation while she fluttered about lavishly, elated for her long-awaited opportunity to shine. Anne Sukie Jackson was also all smiles but for an entirely different reason. Her daughter, Cora, had finally told her the story as she knew it; and, all things notwithstanding, she was tickled pink. *Tee-hee! At long last, the Lord done seen fit to give me a grandchild...and one what even bears my own name.* Meanwhile, the preacher paused and gave them all ample time to stand and be re-seated under the still, watchful, and cautious eye of the white congregation.

When they had all resumed their seats, Assistant Pastor Gabe Ingram gazed admiring at his wife from the pulpit. Molly was sitting on the end of the pew next to Miss Cora, cuddling up to her birth mother, and the two of them were holding hands. Earlier, with the permission of everyone involved, Molly had taken Miss Cora aside before the church service began and told her the whole sordid story. Seeing a picture of *The Shutter-Bug Rapist* and finally getting to know his name proved to be cathartic and fully liberating for Cora. She found great comfort in knowing the whole truth, and a grateful mother and daughter were reunited in love.

Look at my beautiful wife; she is truly amazing! Gabe communed with his own soul. *Things don't always line up just right...and neither do people. The 4-G Crew is certainly a mismatched bunch, but I guess God used Molly's mismatched eyes to see more in us than we could ever have seen in ourselves. Her ability to love and accept us...as well as her own peculiarly mixed-up life...has made this unbelievable day possible. Thank you, Jesus!*

"Back to the point," Pastor Pritchard continued, "I asked her to stand this morning because me and my family want you to know officially, from me and Betsy, that Miss Cora Lee Jackson is our daughter, Molly Anne's…birth mother."

"Whoa!" As soon as that bombshell dropped, there was some uncharacteristic shouting, fainting, and furious hand-fanning going on at The Church of the Evangelicals—the kind that could've rivaled any Sunday morning service at Beulah Bible.

"We won't go into the details of the adoption we made nearly 25 years ago, but suffice it to say, it is now our delight to let the church know that Miss Cora is part of our family, too." The pastor breathed and gave the wilting congregation a chance to do the same. "And while you're digesting that little nugget, I'd like each of you to know that my fine son-in-law, here, and your esteemed assistant pastor, Gabe Ingram, is going on sabbatical from the pulpit."

"Well! Hmph!" This unexpected revelation was met with more than a few sly smirks and tooty-mouthed question marks.

"And before you start trying to put two-and-two together, let me tell you why," the senior pastor said with a grin. "Gabe and Molly are expecting their first child…our first grandchild…and I need not tell you how pleased and happy Betsy and I are. But, in addition to that, Gabe has come up with a wonderful idea for church outreach that is backed by our Elders, the Deacon Board, and the Trustee Board. And I think they're calling it…*Churches United Across the Tracks*…is that right, brothers?" The senior pastor gave a turn and received Gabe's affirming nod.

"But what Gabe will be doing is working with the other churches down in The Presidents to determine what our congregation, along with that of Beulah Bible, can do to help rebuild and support Mount Olive and Holy Ghost Headquarters…because that's what Christians do…we support one another. Amen?"

"Um-hmm—"

The senior pastor's effort at rallying the troops was receiving a spotty reception at best, but he continued undaunted. "With the support of our willing congregation, I've been assured by our very capable Trustee Board...which now, by the way, includes its newest member...Sheriff Bertram Jackson...that we will, in fact, be able to find the much-needed funding for this church rebuilding program. Isn't that right, Greg Allen III?" The pastor pointed to him, all smiles. "Since his dad's untimely death, Greg III has taken over as CEO of Allen Textile Mills, Inc., and he's also accepted the big challenge of stepping into his daddy's shoes, right here, as our Chairman of the Trustee Board." The preacher's face bloomed into a chuckle. "Because Greg III has promised me that he can, in fact, get blood out of a turnip. Isn't that right, Greg III? Please stand."

Greg III did as he was told. He offered the congregation a nerdy bow, aware that no one was the wiser that the new CEO of Allen Textile Mills, Inc. was a black man. Greg III finally understood his daddy's staunch policies on treating all of his employees fairly and with dignity—both black and white. As a result, he not only planned *not* to dismantle his father's policies, which he had once held in such derision, but to enhance them to provide even greater opportunities for people of color in honor of his beloved mother. No one else may ever know, but he would never forget that he was no longer a white racist but a proud black man—proud of his daddy for having the courage to marry the only woman he ever truly loved, even when the whole world was stacked up against them; proud of his mother for accepting the consequences of their love; and thankful to God for giving him this new lease on life. And although he knew it would take a lifetime for him to take it all in, he was very grateful to have the 4-G Crew—and Molly—by his side. And as such, his first order of business was to promote his long-time, loyal employee, Mrs. Anne Sukie Jackson—Molly's grandmother.

In the audience, clocking in with the loudest applause, sat none other than the newest member of The Church of the Evangelicals and a flagship member of the *Churches United Across the Tracks* rebuilding team—Chief Deputy Gus McVey. He had rededicated his life to building up what he and the 4-G Crew had torn down. His mind was made up, even if the people he'd left behind would never understand. *My sister, Molly, says, "Some folk will love you, and some folk will hate you...for the exact same reason...so, let 'em!" And with those mismatched eyes of hers, she's had a lifetime of dealing with that brand o' foolishness. She should know, and I'll take her word for it!*

Greene Jones, the Radio Man, was proud to be sitting alongside his friend, Gus, in the sanctuary. Although not a church member himself, Greene had agreed to do a fundraiser for the combined church rebuilding effort at his radio station—WSCR. He was fully committed to the work and happy to cheer along his buddies. After all, the entire 4-G Crew was back together again, and they were the only real family he'd ever known. *And it's all thanks to Molly. Because of her love and understanding, we can all act like human beings again!*

Deputy Assa Leckie was also in the congregation that Sunday morning as a member of the *Churches United Across the Tracks* rebuilding team which, unbeknownst to him, was the brainchild of the 4-G Crew. He was there simply because by a vote of 3-0, Pastor Renfrow, Bishop Pride, and Pastor Shaundra Strong had selected him to be the point person for the black churches in The Presidents. Assa had traded his uniform that morning for a snazzy, navy-blue suit with a prestigious shirt and tie, and his handsome, vanilla-latte face was smoothly shaven. He'd also set aside his service cap, and his mound of sandy-colored, silky waves was on full display. His piercing, hazel eyes were absorbing every inch of the sanctuary. Assa was none too proud of his coloring since he'd never known his daddy or the origins of his birth, but he'd always been too much of a gentleman to press his mother for the details.

Deputy Assa Leckie had also decided against turning over the G-initial he'd found to the Property Clerk. It had been lying next to the gas can at the botched fire scene at Beulah Bible. Since there had been no fingerprints, Leckie figured the would-be culprit had worn gloves. And he knew that without any other supporting evidence, the isolated G-initial he'd stumbled across was little more than a lost trinket. *No fingerprints. No evidence.* After all, Beulah Bible hadn't been damaged—no real crime had actually been committed. And with the combined-church rebuilding initiative underway, Mount Olive and Holy Ghost Headquarters would fare even better than they had before the fires. He'd make sure of that. *You may get by, white mon, but you not get away.*

As a bit of added insurance, Deputy Leckie had added the G-initial to his own keychain and displayed it often for Chief Deputy Gus McVey to see—and for any of his potential accomplices to know—that he was watching. *I do know that Jesus the Christ can change the spots, even of the leopard...for He did indeed change mine.* Deputy Leckie mused as he sat quietly in the pews of the big white church on that very momentous Sunday morning. *But I do be watching, mon. I be...always...watching.*

****

"And such were some of you: but ye are washed,
but ye are sanctified, but ye are justified
in the Name of the Lord Jesus,
and by the Spirit of our God."
~1 Corinthians 6:11

Other Books by the Author
JEANETTA BRITT

Exciting Fiction

Pickin' Ground (The Lottie Series—Book One)
In Due Season (The Lottie Series—Book Two)
Lottie (The Lottie Series—Book Three)
Empty Envelope
W.O.O.F (Women of Overcoming Faith)
Living in the Seventh Day
Dipped in the Fire (The Fire Series—Book One)
Double-Dipped in the Fire (The Fire Series—Book Two)
Girl with the Mismatched Eyes

Inspiring Poetry

Glimpses (poems of praise)
The Collection (poems of praise)
Flittin' & Flyin' (poems on death, birth & life)
Under the Influence—Spoken Praise
Poems From the Fast
Reunion
Third Ear

Join Jeanetta online:

www.jbrittbooks.com
www.Facebook.com/Jeanetta Britt
www.Facebok.com/JBrittBooks
www.Twitter.com/@JBrittBooks
www.Amazon.com/Jeanetta Britt
www.bn.com/Jeanetta Britt

****

"For whosoever shall call upon
the name of the Lord shall be saved."
~Romans 10:13

ABOUT THE AUTHOR

Jeanetta Britt is a bestselling author who graduated with honors from Fisk University and The University of Michigan. Her passion for writing contemporary Christian Fiction novels—filled with lots of juicy drama and suspense—as well as, Gospel poetry, surfaced in 1996 and has grown steadily since that time. "While being swept up in the story," Jeanetta says, "I want my readers to *feel* the love of Jesus and take refuge in Him, like I did."

After completing a rewarding career in public administration in Dallas, Texas, Jeanetta returned to her native Alabama to write and to live. Her southern roots are reflected in her strong imagery, memorable characters, and delightfully witty storytelling style. She is a sought-after inspirational speaker, by youth and adults alike, with nine novels and seven books of poetry to her credit.

Jeanetta is also an avid gardener and community advocate, and she founded Twelve Stones CDC—a non-profit organization that operates two community gardens in rural Alabama. "We provide free, fresh food for our community and an opportunity for our youth and senior citizens to form vital intergenerational connections, and to get some free exercise, companionship and sunshine, too," she says. "No rules—just love!"

:can be obtained
.com

0623
0006B/137

9 781732 707153